UNDERGROUND

Mudrooroo

ETT IMPRINT

Exile Bay

This edition published by ETT Imprint, Exile Bay 2021

First published by Angus & Robertson 1999
First electronic edition ETT Imprint 2017

ETT IMPRINT

PO Box R1906

Royal Exchange NSW 1225 Australia

ISBN 978-1-925706-00-0 (ebook)
ISBN 978-1-922473-53-0 (pback)

Cover: Schouten Island, Tasmania by Leseur
Cover design by Tom Thompson

Mudrooroo was born in Narrogin in Western Australia in 1938. He travelled extensively throughout Australia and the world and lived in Nepal for ten years, then spent the last ten years of his life in Brisbane. He died on January 14 2020. Mudrooroo had been active in Aboriginal cultural affairs, was a Member of the Aboriginal Arts Unit committee of the Australia Council, and a co-founder with Jack Davis of the Aboriginal Writers, Oral Literature and Dramatists Association. He piloted Aboriginal literature courses at Murdoch University, the University of Queensland, the University of the Northern Territory and Bond University. Mudrooroo was a prolific writer of poetry and prose and is best known for his novels, *Wildcat Falling* and *Master of the Ghost Dreaming;* and his critical work, *Writing from the Fringe. Old Fellow Poems* and *Wildcat Falling* are both available with his audio presentation. His last books were the novel *Balga Boy Jackson* in 2017, and the first volume of his memoirs, *Tripping with Jenny* in 2020.

Books by Mudrooroo available in ETT Imprint

Tripping with Jenny
Balga Boy Jackson
Wildcat Falling (ebook)
Doin' Wildcat
Wildcat Screaming (ebook)
Dr Wooreddy's Prescription for Enduring
   the Ending of the World
Long Live Sandawarra
The Indigenous Literature of Australia
The Garden of Gethsemane
An Indecent Obsession (ebook)
Aboriginal Mythology
The Kwinkan (ebook)
The Secret of Hanging Rock
Old Fellow Poems (ebook)
An Indecent Obsession (ebook)

Master of the Ghost Dreaming series:
Bk 1: The Master of the Ghost Dreaming
Bk 2: The Undying
Bk 3: Underground
Bk 4: The Promised Land

To my dear wife Janine.

"We danced roundabout ... dressed in our breechcloths and academic sashes with all the animals and ghosts under the redwood trees ... The fogdogs laughed and barked from the rim."

Gerald Vizenor

CHAPTER ONE

Don't look askance at me, I was one of the first to reach these goldfields and dig for the metal. Yes, I may not be of your colour, but we're all the same underneath – or are we? Still, what does it matter when the night's fallen like a thick blanket over the diggings and there's nothing much to do until the dawn comes in with a scramble and the heaving of dry dust, and you cough and cough and you wonder what you're doing. But you all know that, don't you? Just adigging, just adigging for the precious metal.

See these two bits of stick, how smooth and worn they are. Real native artefacts. Listen to the sound, how clear it rings. Crack-crack. You know, they belonged to my 'once father'. 'Once father', I'll get to that in due course, for there's a bit of old England in me, and how it got there, well, I'll make it part of my yarn if the darkness holds up.

I'm here to entertain you, to make the night slide away easy and not too slow, for I know you're raring to get at those slugs of metal and collect enough to flee this desolate country where the willy-willies swirl up the dust until you curse the day you thought to roam – to here, where time hangs heavy on your minds and you get to thinking of the girl you left behind. Maybe, eh? Well, I remember a girl, but she left me behind. Left me behind: a stranger in a strange land. I don't hail from these parts. Who does? Just a blow-in like the rest of you lot. I come from far to the south east, from an island and now I've become a nomad, a wanderer seeking to find fortune. Strike it rich and we'll all be home, eh?

Strike it rich! We roam the earth afire with our quest, with our thirst. Drifters, driven here and there by idle rumours, and when the colour's gone from the soil and the big companies come in to rip deep into the guts of the earth, following down that reef which we just pecked at on the surface, well, we up stakes and off we wander seeking always that lode of gold at the end of the rainbow. Wandering, that's what we're good at; but then the land's wide enough for our roaming and there's gold for the taking if you get in first or second. Hear tell there's another strike far to the north, gold for the picking rather than the digging. A mob upped their stakes, packed their swags and lit out for there just the other day where, I hear, it ain't dry all the year round; every six months or so there comes a mighty flood, just like in the Bible, and when the water subsides there shines the gold. Well, Noah was a nomad too and he circumnavigated the whole globe, just sailing, sailing on that wooden boat of his which didn't handle too well against the wind, so he drifted rather than sailed her hard; but when the flood went down, he saw the glitter of that gold shining, telling him to leave his ark and rejoice at his strike, for it was the mother lode.

Well, like old Noah I left a ship, though I didn't rejoice at leaving her. She rather left me, falling apart from under, so to speak, and I was washed up on these shores. Been in the west a long time now, following the strikes from the south to the east and soon it'll be north for me. But, you know, there's times when the ocean surges in my brain and I've got to head for her and gaze across the waters, remembering that long ago voyage much as you might recall that day you took to the gold trail, much as I dream recall that voyage my friend's mother made on a shit of a ship. That still rankles in me, but never mind, it wasn't our mother, was it; but still I feel her suffering as I stare over the tumbling waves and feel the wheel again quivering in my hands like a live thing, and female at that. It's then that I think of forsaking this land and getting on a vessel with a course set towards the pole star, maybe a brig, not one of those ones that now go charging through the waves, battering them down where once we danced light as a feather.

Yeah, they say we're in the age of steam and iron. Well, let that be, I still prefer the old ways, which once were new to me. Get on some craft under full canvas and sail north west. Up there lies Africa, and did not the Queen of Sheba come from that continent laden with gold for that old Israelite, Solomon, who it's been said was a bit of a wiseacre in his time. Gold there just for the collecting, at least that's what I've heard and the voice is getting louder and louder. Once, you know, I had a friend from there and never once did he mention this yellow metal. Yeah, but he was worth his weight in gold to us. He was one of those Africans. Caught, enslaved, fought and escaped, and became a hero of sorts before he took to the sea and became a sailor, sailing, sailing over that lonesome ocean. Guess he's on her still, between one port or another ...

He was our chief mate, not so much a captain which means something less than chief in our language. Well, he was the one that guided us as we sailed from the east on the ill-fated voyage which would eventually fling me up here, in this place where the dust demons roam, though I'm a bit of a devil myself and cannot abide the day. Still, forget that and just hold a picture of that schooner scudding along. Beautiful, isn't she? A trim craft, saucy and dancehall smart, who could kick up her heels and lift her skirts high as she skipped across the ocean. A regular Lola Montez, until her bottom got too heavy with the barnacles and weeds. Still, she was as bonny a vessel as I've ever been on and charitable as well for she took all of us on without a protest and carried us on and on, ever westwards as we searched, much like those Jewish people travelling out of Egypt, for a promised land. We were like those Greeks too, them that sailed off to fight a war and then got lost on the way home. Yeah, ours was like the voyage of that Ulysses. It went on and on, though at the end there was nary a glimpse of home, let alone a promised land.

Well, it took a long time to get to where we were going. And what was that promised land I found myself in? This place, with its dust, with its flies that seek even me out, and dare I mention that awful sun which sheers away at my very skin, flesh and bone. You blokes, you diggers, y'know I lost my mob along with that schooner and too often do I imagine our mob in spirit up among those stars where the silver ocean glimmers – and there they are on that bonny vessel breasting the milky waves as they sail on, searching always for that promised land, our home away from home and perhaps on some planet where our ancestors sit and forget the dreadful doings on this earth.

Well, you've had enough of dust and heat, I dare say, and need a tale about the far cold southern ocean with its icebergs and strange werebears lurching above the snow, with its squalls and tempests and phantom ships petrified in strange frozen waves that take away the living temperature and render the whole crew, captain down to cabin scruff, stiff and dead. It's cold, mates, cold as the death you dream as the sweat trickles down your backs and stirs the hairs as if you feel a phantom touch of a frozen hand belonging to someone who once loved you ...

No thanks, I don't need that sort of drink to soften up my pipes. They say that grog is a curse to folks like me, but I have found other tastes curse enough. So now, to set the mood, hear these sticks sounding like spoons as I make the rhythm for this bit of verse.

They made of me
A ghost down under
Made for me a place to plunder,
Yeah, to plunder
Way down under,
Pardon me while I chunder.

Not so bright is it, but then neither is this night with the sky all obscured from the dust of your dryblowing. Perhaps I should give you 'Roaming in the Gloaming'; but well, I don't know what a gloaming is. What? Dusk y'say. Well, you learn a new word every day. Now another song to set the mood of our gloomy tale.

Our vessel was a doughty one
It ploughed the seas alone
And we huddled on the deck
And wished not to be a wreck
So far away from home, boys,
So far away from home, me boys.

Our captain, he was as black
As the startling thunder clap
He was as restless as the lightning And
struck out along with the wrack Along
with the wrack, me boys Alone with the
wrack.

Well, that's more rousing than that old ghost dirge, though what is the night fit for, but the telling of ghostly yarns and phantom ships and ghoulies which wait for the shipwrecked sailor. Worse, I hear tell, is what lurks for you at the bottom of the sea, where the dead men swing in the currents and fish have lights in their heads to navigate about them. Remember those old, old stories of Ulysses and Jason. They heard the sirens singing and met ancient Neptune who had an underwater kingdom and loved you or hated you, saved you or drowned you, whatever took his fancy at the time. Never met him, though I've seen more than mortal men. Strange female things just as mean and bad as those sirens enticing men with their singing, along with their billowing tits and flowing hair, though not their fishy tails, what use are those?

One of those sort it was that got into our chief mate's brain and swung him away from us. He was never again one with us in spirit. It was then, about the time he changed, that he took it into his head to give our vessel a name. He called her the *Kore,* upsetting most of our mob who wanted a different vision. But he had ill-luck covering him and from him it spread so that we began to think that we were all doomed. All this happened after we had come upon a wreck that had been cursed from the day she sailed. And when she flung herself upon the beach, her curse waited for us to pull up alongside, for we looted her, but then finder's keepers, or so we thought at the time. From then on, something came after us and then our chief mate, our captain, disappeared one night, and my then father and I had to seek him out again with direful consequences. We had to find him! He was the only one who knew how to keep our vessel happy. He rode her hard until she learnt to keep the course, but without him she wallowed slow in the water, fat arsed with weeds and barnacles.

He might have scraped her, but he let her be, for it seemed he had lost his wits along with his luck. He even carved a female shape from a log. Said it was to be our figurehead. It was then he called our schooner the *Kore.* A kore, a maiden with her fat white breasts on which you could rest a tankard, with flowing locks of yellow hair and evil red glaring eyes that were baleful enough to shatter any rocks and reefs in our way. But, alas, she was no longer our old craft. That wooden witch image possessed her, making her spiteful and mean. She challenged anything that stood in her way just like one of those haughty steamships made of iron, and like one of them her end came abrupt and sudden; but, but, why circle about that when it has nothing to do with the red maw of fright.

No, it is not part of this yarn into which I settle, as I lean back and gather what seems a breath. Relax, relax! The night is young and randy enough for us to take our time. She'll enjoy more than her luck deserves, and with her cooling down will come a dew to lower the dust, so if your mug is empty, fill it. Drink up, mates, there's a coin, gold gleaming, and time as long as the night enduring. Drink! There's rum enough to help the ghoulies creep into my tale.

I'll make it a regular story and begin with those of our mob who stood out from the rest. First, Mungkati, a big blackfellow. His name meant thickhead and he hated it and was easily led astray to take another name. Fada, you see, who did the naming was always one for the latest name of splendour, such as Victoria; but Mungkati could never be a Victoria so he had been called Hercules, which he liked much better, especially when he was given the story to it by Fada who was the bloke who one day arrived on our southern island with a mission to save us from devils such as himself. He saved us all right. He got us all together on a God-forsaken bit of rock where we quickly began to pine away. We blamed it on evil spirits who had been waiting for this opportunity to get us and so did Fada who battled to stop them from harming us. One of his subterfuges was renaming us so that the demons would be bamboozled. This didn't help at all, and so he left us on that piece of rock while he went off to write a report on us which he had published as *The Great Reconciliation.* In it, he was the chief character and we were poor victims with hands upheld for succour. (There was no mention that we had stolen his schooner and went off in her.) But all this is another story and he doesn't figure that much in this yarn, though he has turned up here to make the goldfields his home.

Well, I'll tell you a bit about him. He is what is called a philanthropist and is a most Christian gentleman. You all know him, the Leader of the Legislative Council. Yes, good Sir George and there is even talk that he is to be our next governor. A local man is needed and there are those who say he will get things done for this colony, and as evidence will point to the church he got built here. As I've said, a most Christian gentleman, though he has a piratical side. Well, he did when he was master over us and also had a liking for what he called the stories of the old paganism and since he considered some of us still pagans, he gleefully gave those ones heathen names: Jason, Hector, Hercules and others I can't recall, together with the promise that when the offenders had reconciled themselves to the Christian faith they too would be given proper names. I was a child then and baptized as George and this has remained with me. The others never used what they considered their 'ghost' names, for they saw white-skinned ones such as your good selves, as ghosts; but as I've said Mungkati became known as Hercules for ever more. So I'm George, named after the then reigning monarch and not after himself, even though Jangamuttuk my supposed father had declared: 'He's the king of the castle, and he's a dirty rascal.' I knew the English words, but being a kid what they were hinting at passed over me as did the laughter when Fada was coupled with 'black velvet'.

Well, all this naming business happened a year before the King carked it and Her Majesty ascended the throne. God save Victoria, though I cannot help but wonder what I would have been called if I had been born from her, so to speak. Victor or Victoria, or just Albert. He did and still does, that Fada, that Sir George, like the sound of royal names, even storybook ones. Why, he even called my mother, Lalla Rookh, some fabulous queen of oriental splendour, he assured her as he took his pleasure.

Anyway, Mungkati, or Hercules, was a big fellow with a big temper to match and when it overpowered him he hit out with what came to hand. One time, he even did a fellow in with an axe and I'll tell you why later, but for now just imagine that axe flashing down upon your head. How it strikes with a sodden thud, digging in deep, clefting the skull in twain. Bits of bone and brain flying everywhere. The blood gushing out a regular torrent. Some drops splatter on your face and your tongue darts out to lick the ruby fluid. It tastes of copper with a subtle flavour of rum; but I get beyond myself. I am harmless and it is only the darkness of the night which brings such thoughts to mind, for I did not do the deed, but thickheaded Mungkati/Hercules did with his infernal temper. He split his man and splattered us with the gore of blood guilt for ever more.

Well that was Hercules, so unlike our chief mate, the African. He was a different sort of bloke – one who in his day had seen and had his share of cruelty. You know, he began his life as a baby born in the cramped confines of a slaver ship. He entered this world as his fellows died and rotted about him. Born on that ship, he never had a feeling for the solid earth of a land he could call his own, though perhaps he yearned for it. They sold him in the Americas, but always there was the call of the restless waters in his veins. Now he is out there this night, battling the elements somewheres; but enough of him we called *Wadawaka*, Seaborn. Let him rest while you fill your mugs to the brim, for the night is long and the grog is there for the drinking, as long as you've got something in your poke, for my coin is all done. Here's to our chief mate, Seaborn. Lift your mugs high in homage and I break my yarn with a song and you settle back.

> *In these days of old,*
> *When you dig up the gold*
> *And the dust fills up your gob*
> *And you need some grog*
> *To make you believe*
> *You're a damned lucky sod.*

There, there enough of that. Crack-crack, loud enough to wake you and the dead besides eh, these sticks which come from the dead and call the ghoulies down upon us. We need a parson to keep them at bay and we had such a sort on our schooner who had an affinity for such things. Not of your regular sort that dresses in black, his skin was black enough and he was handy with a song and spell when the going got tough and we got scared. Fada named him Orpheus after one of those ancient pagan fellows, but to us he was always *Jangamuttuk*, Ghost Conqueror. Well, like parsons are meant to do, he gave us strength when strength was needed, singing hymns to the land beyond the sun. He had a magic voice that could call the animals to him and even quieten the storms when they were raging, but like that Orpheus fellow, he suffered a similar fate when he sought out our mate to return his mind to him.

And perhaps you need to know of me, George. I stood next to Wadawaka at the helm and relieved him when he sought his bunk. Wadawaka, our African mate, taught me how to judge the schooner's ways. She trembled with life, life that turned evil when he named her the *Kore* and gave her a figurehead. Yes, she was alive and many a time at night when I held the wheel, I felt her timbers twist under the touch of my hands and emit a ghastly groaning as she ripped apart the pellucid, placid sea.

And what and who were the rest, you may want to know. Well, our mob was twenty men and women, all that remained of us poor blackfellows after Fada had got through with his conciliating. Wadawaka it was who taught the men to furl and unfurl the sails and other things which were necessary to keep us on our course. The women, when our shrouds grew tattered and fluttered in the wind like deadmen's rags, sewed them together again so that they might hold the wind. We kept her going towards the west, and as other voyagers we had adventures along the way, some of which were weird and strange. Now raise your pannikins high and toast all those who put to sea, while I finish off with a song my erstwhile father used to sing:

> They made for us
> A land to plunder
> a land to plunder
> Way down under.

CHAPTER TWO

The winds had been favourable when we left our island, blowing constantly from the east. They endured for a number of days, then fell away, replaced by spates of southerly squalls which drove us to the land. After some days when these had blown themselves out, we put to sea on an easterly. Our schooner was in good spirits and we raced to the west until the fickle wind reversed itself to force her back on her wake. Worse, this signalled the change of the season and the westerly came down on us laden with a bitter cold, draping our vessel's rigging in hoar frost. We fashioned cloaks from our blankets, covering them with the skins of kangaroos and wallabies which Wadawaka had collected when we had had to shelter on the mainland. Before, an adventure had erupted about us, we had filled our time with hunting and this now served us well. Our skin-coated blankets kept us somewhat warm, but as the adverse wind continued and the cold endured, most ·of our mob took refuge below decks, where they huddled miserably in the tiny space and complained bitterly.

There was little that we could do. The wind rose into a gale which blasted us back on our course. Wadawaka let the vessel run before it. She didn't like it that much and slumped along with her head bent low. Every now and again, the knitting needles she had thrust through her hair bobbed and weaved and we might have ended back where we had begun if the gale had not fallen away to a steady wind. She stopped her pitching and yawing, and the deck stayed horizontal. It was some time after this that a man poked his hairy head out of a hatchway, waited for a while as if he did not believe that the world had indeed settled down, then finding that it had, he pulled his weighty body through and onto the deck. He stood there slightly swaying, staring at the white-capped sea with a scowl of dislike.

Although Wadawaka was a big man, this blackfellow towered over him. It was Hercules, who looked like some bulky bear in his hairy cloak. I was standing beside Wadawaka and watched as the giant bear bent down and pulled out his huge waddy, his constant companion. His beard and hair were unkempt and streamed in the wind as he stood before us, muttering fiercely before bellowing: 'We have had enough of this pitching and rolling. We need the firm earth beneath our feet and the warmth of a campfire to unfreeze our bones.'

Wadawaka stared into his glowering features, then replied with a shrug. 'What could I do, when the wind howled in her icy rigging and she turned and scurried east. Well, since the tempest has lessened his fury, we'll run close to the shore in the hopes of finding sheltered anchorage in the lee of an island, then we'll go ashore.'

Hercules hefted his club and grimaced at the waves as if he would batter them down. The challenge was accepted and a huge wave rose to curve over our stern. As it did so, the giant jumped through the hatchway and dragged the cover across. The wave crashed down and we were tumbled about and along the deck. Luckily, we fell into the bow of the schooner and so escaped being washed overboard. When we had scrambled to our feet, we saw that the sea had spent its fury and now rippled gently beneath our hull.

Wadawaka took the helm from me and corrected our course so that the wind came from the starboard. Our single sail shivered and swung to take it up. The sea was still the gentle ripple; but the waves came from the sides and strangely were translated into a harsh rocking of our hull. From below came groans as a new misery was added to their suffering.

'Well, if they want to land, they have to endure it,' Wadawaka said with a puzzled look on his face, for how could such a calm sea set us to such a rocking? He turned the wheel a fraction and the vessel pitched and shuddered so that even he had difficulty keeping his feet. 'Must be some sort of current,' he said as he struggled with the wheel. From below came the sound of retching and my stomach turned over in sympathy. Wadawaka the Seaborn showed no sign of being unduly upset at the motion, though the swirling waters about the schooner had discoloured a large patch of the sea.

The long coastline emerged, covered with clouds which wept a light drizzle of tears. Wadawaka managed to alter the course so that the wind took us away from the mud-coloured patch of ocean. As we left its confines, our schooner eased her rolling and she trembled only slightly. 'Ah, she too wants to rest against the land,' our chief mate smiled as he let his body move with her vibrations. He eased her towards a point of land which was shaped like the head of a lizard. As we came nearer, the head fattened out into a plump body.

'Well, we have reached a lizard of an island,' Wadawaka exclaimed. 'And there is the tail!' At the very tip, he swung the wheel to bring us about. Our sail flapped, then tugged us in a different direction. 'Now let's see what is on the lee,' he muttered. 'Ah, there's a bay between tail and body, it will be our resting place. Take us there, now girl.'

In obedience, the schooner slid into the bay.

'Drop the sail, George,' Wadawaka called. 'I'll lash the helm and then let go the anchor.'

Sheltered from the wind, our schooner seemed to sigh as she rode at peace. The light rain continued to fall, making the beach hazy and misty. It was then that Hercules leapt up on deck and gave a shout. Then most of our mob emerged to gaze at the shore. I looked at the woebegone lot. It hadn't been fun being confined in the womb of the vessel; but the sight of land would quickly revive their spirits. And it did! They had had enough of ships and oceans and quickly unroped the boat which had been lashed to the deck and heaved it over the side. With a boat hook I held her close as Hercules and four men, bulky in their cloaks, gingerly clambered down then rowed off to reconnoitre the beach – although perhaps they might have waited for their shaman, my father Jangamuttuk, to go along with them, for who would negotiate the right of landing if there was another tribe of blackfellows living there. Hercules' idea of negotiation was to knock out any opposition with his club; but what was a waddy against a spear or musket?

Wadawaka let them go without a word of protest. He had a healthy respect for the physical prowess of Hercules, but none for his mental abilities. Still, concerned about such a dash into the unknown, he lifted his telescope and carefully examined the island. He held it where the land rose up towards a central ridge. Even without the aid of the glass, I could see a small, square log cabin nestling in a hollow. 'Someone there,' he said, 'not blackfellows either. There's a garden about the hut and what seems to be corn growing. Well, we'll wait a bit and let Hercules handle it. He'll either get his fool head blown off, or bash someone's head in.'

It was then that a musket shot sounded. A darker vapour marked the grey mist of rain in front of the cabin and then a figure came to the doorway. He calmly reloaded his long musket, but kept the butt resting between his legs. He looked at our mob who in turn eyed him. He stayed in his doorway not even bothering to raise his gun. After a few minutes of stalemate, Hercules and the men with him backed to the boat and pushed it off into the surf. They scrambled into it and hastily rowed for the schooner. It seemed that Hercules for once had decided that more than his club was necessary to break the deadlock. Perhaps we needed ghost weapons, I thought, dashing below to find my pistol. I checked its priming, then thrust it in my belt where it was hidden beneath my cloak.

When I came back on deck, I saw the boat pulling alongside and Wadawaka flinging down an armful of spears. I wondered why he hadn't taken a couple of the muskets we had, but held my peace. Jangamuttuk, my father, now managed to make it up from below. The poor old fellow had suffered dreadfully from seasickness and was still shaky on his pins.

Still, he wanted to go ashore and so I held the boat close to our vessel's side while Wadawaka picked him up and deposited him in it. Even though it was now a tight squeeze, we ourselves then scrambled down. As we rowed towards the shore, each sweep of the oars threatened to swamp our overloaded dinghy.

Still, Wadawaka steadied himself enough to use his telescope. He passed it to me as a wave rose under us. As we rose higher and higher, I held the glass to my eye and trained it on the figure. It was indeed one of those we called ghosts, but clad in rough clothing similar to our own. He wore pants and a jacket made out of kangaroo skins with the fur inside. His grey hair hung lank about a face mostly covered with a grey beard from which a single blue eye gleamed balefully. The other, if he had one, was covered by a black patch. On his head he wore a possum skin which still held the head poking out above his forehead.

Suddenly, the eye piece of the telescope slammed into my eye as the wave broke. The boat shuddered and went under. It struggled up and then grounded. We scrambled out and as we pulled our craft up onto the beach, the ugly ghost shouted: 'You lot, beware! This is my island and there's only room enough for me.' He lifted his long musket and aimed it towards us. This caused us to huddle about the boat, all except for Wadawaka, and Jangamuttuk who had revived once his feet had touched solid earth.

'We're coasting westwards,' Wadawaka shouted, 'but the wind's agin us. We have to wait it out here. When it's for us, we'll be away. No problems with that, is there?'

'Well, you are not much welcome,' the ghost shouted. 'From the looks of you, you're not government or free booters such as myself. You got a fine vessel there; but who's in charge of her? You blackfellows can hardly paddle a canoe, let alone sail a schooner. Where's your captain? I'll have a word with him, for I bid you welcome only as long as you keep the peace.'

'We blackfellows crew and sail this schooner,' Wadawaka shouted back. 'You've never been to the West Indies where we do all the work, the sailing and the piloting and a right good job we make of it. Far better than some of them whiteskins that now rest on the bottom of the sea. They bandied words about our ability or lack of it.'

'Well, it's the first I've seen of it along these shores and I've been here from the first,' rejoined the apparition. 'You lot don't seem to be West Indians anyways. More likely from that big island to the south east. I know them blackfellows or what remains of them as that's where I started out, courtesy of Her Majesty's Government. Anyway, find a spot to camp;

but away from my cabin, and mind you leave my garden alone. Hard enough it was to get the seeds and then the plants to grow. There's enough stealing from bandicoots and the like without you lot helping yourselves to them. Anyway get settled, and when you've had a feed of your own grub and got your land legs back, I'll come down and hear out your tale. Sure enough, it's indeed a worthy schooner you've got there, and run by blackfellows,' he added, his glowing eye fixed on her. Then with his head nodding, setting the possum head bobbing, he disappeared back into his cabin.

Hercules snarled as the sound came to us of the door being slammed then barred. He stared at the closed door and growled: 'Who wants to be cooped up with that. They stink and can't keep their hands off our women. I've seen that creep somewheres before and I'll remember in time. Well, he'll keep. Let's find a place to set up camp. I can't stand this weepy rain that clings to your hair until it gets too heavy, then trickles down your neck.'

'You find a spot,' Wadawaka agreed. 'I'll go and get one of the spare sails. We don't need a *koorowri*, a hut, but only the framework for a *wooloa*.'

I went with Wadawaka to the boat and helped him to push it into the water and then row out to our vessel. The rest of our mob took themselves ashore while we got the sail, a large pot and tin cups, some of our provisions, flour and salt tack. We stacked them into the boat which was waiting for us with the last of our people.

Back on shore, we found that Hercules had decided to set up camp in a thicket of small trees that grew in a shallow hollow some distance from the cabin. A number of saplings with forked tips had been cut which then had been hammered into the ground upright in a line. In the forks were placed horizontal poles and then others were propped along these at an angle of 45 degrees. We flung the canvas over this and fastened down the back with stones. It made a long open-fronted tent and protected us from the drizzle which still continued to fall. Everything dripped and we wondered where we might find dry kindling to start our fires. I looked across at the ghost's cabin and at the lean-to stacked with short logs and kindling. The door was still tightly closed and as the only windows were to the front it was easy for me and a couple of others to sneak over and get what we wanted. Soon, we had three fires blazing along the long front of our tent and could feel the warmth against our skins. Now Wadawaka got me to fill the iron pot with water. The ghost had chosen his site well and there was a spring close to the cabin. When I returned, my friend had set up two upright forked sticks on opposite sides of a fire. He took the

19

pot of water from me, put a green piece of wood through the handle and hung it over the fire. He flung in a piece of salt pork, then with a shrug went off to look over the garden. He came back with potatoes, beans and corn cobs which he put into the pot. When it came on the boil he pulled away some of the burning logs so that the stew went down to a simmer. After this he flung in some flour and salt and stirred it.

We were sipping the stew from our tin cups, when my mother Ludjee glanced up and gave a short scream. I grabbed for my pistol as she got to her feet and ran towards two women who had crept out of the thicket and were staring at us.

My mother rushed to the two strangers, stopped in front of them and stared wildly from face to face. Suddenly, the three fell to ahugging and both exclaimed, 'Ludjee, Ludjee' over and over again while Mother cried, 'Nadjee, Lorimee,' gazing from one to the other. Now all three began laughing and crying. At last they settled and came to the fire where we were sitting. It was then that I heard that these were my mother's long lost sisters who had been stolen in front of her eyes by a boatload of ghosts, one of whom was the one they were now with. Malone was his name.

Before we had been exiled to the northern island where I had been born, Ludjee and her sisters were living on another island to the west of the mother land. The times were unravelling there as the ghosts had come through to take the mother. The tribe stayed on, waiting and wondering how things would turn out and if the times would ever again become aligned. One day, the three young sisters were sporting in the surf when a whale boat came rowing into the bay. They were used to such watercraft by then and took no notice, continuing their play until it bobbed next to them. 'Come my pretties,' one of the ghosts called, holding out a yellow ribbon, which fluttered in the breeze. Ludjee hung back as her two sisters swam to the boat and taking hold of the side with one hand stretched out the other for the gaudy piece of cloth which flapped in the breeze and eluded their grasping hands. It didn't help that the ghost who held them, kept pulling the ribbons away as they attempted to snatch them. Then before my mother's horrified eyes, while her sisters were distracted, the two men at the stern suddenly grabbed the hands holding onto the boat and heaved them aboard. The boat rocked alarmingly, but did not capsize. Now the ghosts rowed swiftly out of the bay and that was the last my mother had seen of her sisters until this day.

'But how come you stay with that ghost?' she asked them. 'Haven't you tried to get away?'

'He's better than the one we were with,' Nadjee replied. 'He doesn't hurt us like the first brute who had us. Why we were only little girls and he almost split us in half ...'

'How come you got to be with this fellow. He looks evil ...'

'You can't judge a bloke by his looks you know. You mob for example look a rum lot in your furry skins; but then so do we. We look like great lumpy monsters, so give us another hug before I tell you how we became Malone's sluts, for that is what they call us.'

Again the three fell to embracing, then Lorimee took up the story. 'Well,' she said, 'When those ghosts kidnapped us, they took us along the coast. They hoisted their sail and coasted along on a breeze until night fell when they put in to shore and made camp. It was then that they began squabbling over us and the brute that laid claim to us decked an even more loathsome one with an oar. It broke off and he jammed the shattered end into the bloke's throat and leant on it. He guffawed as his mate squirmed and then when he had had enough fun, he jerked the end of the oar out and with it came his life blood. That cowed the others and he got them to bury his victim while he turned to us. They had tied us to a tree with a rope about our necks leaving our legs and hands free. That didn't do us much good, then he got first Nadjee down, then me. He laughed as our tiny fists punched his face, then his own fist soon put a stop to it. When we came to, the last man was *just* finishing off with me. I ached and pained all over and all I could hear as he heaved away was Nadjee groaning softly to herself and then I heard someone else sobbing on and on and it was me. They didn't care if we were sore or bled, and kept at us until we were nigh crippled. If it hadn't been for Malone, we most likely would have ended up dead. We couldn't run off as we could barely walk, and later when our bodies had gotten used to the violation and they had eased off, when we did try to escape, they just about flogged the life out of us. You should see our backs.'

Both sisters pulled off their heavy skin jackets and turned their dark backs towards the fire as if to warm them. The flames seemed to reach out through the misty air to gleam off the criss-crosses of white scars that marked the black. There were gasps from us and then sobs and even the sky wept a gentle rain. Ludjee shed tears as she traced out the pattern of torment and murmured: 'You cannot call them beasts, for never have I met a beast that did such a thing. Surely it is true as those to the north believe that they are *moma*, devils who lack an affinity with humans.'

'Yes and we know how they handled their moma, don't we,' Hercules growled, not shouting for a change. 'I was betrothed to Kaddinee. She was only fourteen and I had to wait and while I was waiting they got her. We could not understand their ferocity as we came across first her head which they had left in a fork of a tree to mock us, then her violated body. They had cut off her breasts, though they had had to scrape along the breast bone for she was a mere child, then hammered a stake between her legs. Well, this ghost or moma will pay!'

His head fell onto his knees and he went quiet as death. There was a feeling of impending violence in the air and Wadawaka tried to lessen it by asking if anyone knew that this ghost had mistreated women.

Nadjee scowled and then spat into the fire. 'He treats us well enough and only now and again makes us go to his mates. It is their way and sometimes when they come and there is a party there is much singing and dancing, and we have a fine time. We are used to it now.'

Lorimee added: 'Where could we go, if we left him and who would take us in? We have been defiled by them and even those blackfellows on the mainland opposite are frightened of us. So we stay, work for him and sometimes party. It's not all bad, though. See that garden and that pile of wood, it's not him that tends the plants or cuts the wood. It's us. He sits around in that hut of his and dips his pannikin into his rum cask and ...'

'He trades us for that rum,' Nadjee exclaimed.

'He's not so bad, not like the others,' Lorimee broke in. 'It was far worse with them. It was lucky for us when he won us, for strangely he likes a bit of the lash himself though you have to be careful not to hurt him, or else he bellows like a stuck pig.'

'Won you?!' Wadawaka exclaimed, as if he was re-living other horrors invoked by the women's story.

'Yes at cards. They were using us, all of them, but only that brute owned us. Malone, our ghost, had taken a fancy to both of us. Even then he had thought of settling on this island and "living the life of Riley" as he put it. This meant that he wanted us to do all the work as well as touching him up with the lash every now and again. So, he waited and seized the opportunity when it came. He got the brute drinking and out came the cards and he finally got us with a couple of red queens which he had palmed.'

'And that's why he calls us the Queen of Spades and Clubs,' Nadjee broke in, 'though he got us with the red, but he says that it was the black that made him lucky and when he gets into a game these days, he rubs our skins for luck. '

'To get back to what happened next,' Lorimee raised her voice above that of her sister, 'that brute, he let us go just like that, saying that there were more birds in the bush and he only liked to sample them, not own them.'

'True,' Nadjee regained the story. 'Just like that, but that Malone once said that he was off to some place up the coast and didn't need to be lumbered with two black women.'

'Well,' Lorimee said, 'whatever made him do it, he did it and that was good for us.'

Wadawaka picked up a glowing stick from the fire and flung it out into the darkness. He watched. A tiny flame flickered up, then disappeared. 'You know,' he said, 'it is the same everywhere for us black folks. The whip, the lash, manacles and degradation. It is too much and ...' Suddenly he broke off, staring hard into the gathering darkness. Such was the intensity of his gaze that we all began looking into the blurred outline of a tree where something, light and indistinct fluttered among the leaves. Then it was gone and all that we could think was that some spirit had been listening to the women's tale of woe.

Wadawaka, more agitated than he had been when he was speaking, got to his feet and prowled within the illumination of the campfires, stopping every now and again to stare off into the gathering darkness. At least the drizzle had stopped and now as night fell like a heavy blanket, the clouds parted to let the moon peer down. It was a half moon with a halo, surrounded by the brittle sparks of stars. These made me think of the skyworld and the campfires of our ancestors, though then I became frightened as I imagined ghosts as numerous as falling drops of rain flooding down to conquer this world of ours. This was what my father and our shaman had told us and it was under his influence that we had begun our voyage westwards so that we might be free of them once and for all.

I missed my friend and got to my feet. I was about to follow him, for it was not good to leave a person to wander by himself in a strange land, when there was another disturbance as the ghost Malone walked into our camp with a small barrel on his shoulder. He smelt of rancid meat and rum and in the fire and moonlight did indeed appear like some demon. He stopped, jerked his head about and saw my mother's sisters there.

'Didn't I tell you to stay in the bush until I called for you,' he snarled at them. 'Just remember who you belong to and what blackfellows think of you for being with me. Queens or traitors, eh? You're better off here with me than with a bunch of damn savages anyway. So keep yourselves to yourselves and stick by me, or else,' he threatened.

The two women glanced at each other, then back at their ghost and Nadjee muttered: 'Why, are you going to whip us?'

They made no attempt to get to their feet and Malone licked his lips as he stared at them before shrugging and muttering: 'They're like dogs, you know, like dogs.' His one good eye gleamed malignantly as it flicked from face to face. 'Treat 'em with kindness, let 'em sleep at the foot of your bed, throw 'em a few scraps, avoid their sharp teeth if they get stroppy and you got friends for life. Can't get rid of 'em, you know. Malone's sluts and they know their master and I could show you how much they can show it ...' He stopped abruptly with a leer, licking his lips as if he was about to go on, then clamped his mouth shut as if he had just recollected who he was among, a mob of blackfellows, some of whom most likely understood English and might take his words amiss.

He covered what confusion he felt, if any, by setting the cask down carefully, then flopping down next to it. He seemed not to notice that we were all staring at him with hostility and instead pulled out a pannikin, fiddled with the cask until he got the bung out, let his mug fill then shut off the flow and gulped the liquid down. As his face lifted and dropped with the emptying of the mug, I noticed that his possum cap had two red stones in the place of eyes and these stared venomously at me, reminding me of other eyes, of another ghost who had treated me with kindness, if it could be called that. I didn't like thinking about that and turned my attention to Malone's one blue eye which was clouded over as if with some filmy tissue, and if the eye beneath the black patch was in similar condition, it meant that he was going blind and needed workers or companions.

Now, drunkenly he muttered something indistinctly, hawked a mass of phlegm up, spat it into the fire where it sizzled a long moment, then spoke again. 'Well, at least one of you knows the English language and I expect all of you'll know what the government will do to you, if they catch you with that boat. As far as I know blacks are property and with not as much up in the top storey as we white fellows. You need a white bloke in charge of you, tell you what to do and how to do it. You'll get by that way and no-one'll say a word against you. Well, I'm glad to know that you can sail this sort of boat, I can't, but what's the use of sailing her if you can't put into a port. As I've said, what you need is a white man in charge, then bob's your uncle. Look at me, I'm that white bloke and what's more I've got a load of kangaroo skins waiting to be taken and sold. You've got the boat and I've got the colour. A fair swap if you ask me. Nothing else to say, except let's celebrate your new captain and he's a kind master as long as you don't get in his way. Ask the queens there. I'm a good bloke. Never laid a finger on them though they've deserved it more than once and sometimes, you know, I need a bit of a massage and they go at it too hard just out of spite. Well, that's neither here nor there. So what do you say, eh? There's nothing but desert to the west of us, best if we load up the skins, go east then north to sell 'em at Port Jackson.'

Hercules gave a snarl which if the ghost had known him would have put him on guard. He didn't, nor did he heed the fact that the giant had been dangerously silent. When Hercules was like that it was best to get him talking, but Malone ignored him and we weren't butting in to warn him. Now the ghost swung his filmy eye over us as he babbled on. 'Of course, we'll have to get ourselves presentable. Get you and me cleaned up. When you got a vessel like this, you got to look the part, swank it up a bit.'

He gulped his rum and it was then that Hercules lumbered to his feet and went out of the firelight. I thought that he was going for a piss and this got me wondering about our missing chief mate. What would he make of the ghost's idea? It was an easy answer. He would think it shit. It was then that Hercules returned. He took two large steps as he came into the firelight and stood in front of the ghost. His arm swung back, then down. The axe which he had taken from Malone's woodpile flashed down, through the possum skin cap and then the brain, cleaving the skull in twain as it lodged up against the top of the spine. Bits of bone and grey matter splattered over us. The women shrieked and the two sisters rushed to the dead ghost and began wailing: 'He wasn't that bad; he wasn't that bad,' they cried over and over again.

In fascination I watched the blood gush from the split skull. How red and intoxicating it looked. I felt like rushing in and lapping it up. I was on my feet ready to go to the dying ghost and press my mouth over his red gaping wound, when I got ahold of myself. Murder had been done and where was my father, Jangamuttuk. Where was Wadawaka? In a panic I rushed away to find them, for they would know what to do.

CHAPTER THREE

I raced away from the camp in the direction I had seen Wadawaka go. For some reason, my rush inland soon faltered until I was only walking slowly through the scrubby bush under an eerie moon, which made me feel that I was moving in sorrow through that awful graveyard which Fada had laid out to hold our bodies after he had stolen what souls he could. Then, as if in a trance state in which everything appears at a distance before it strikes, I saw a dark figure standing motionless on the edge of a shining pool of water. I slowed even more, for who knew what things in the guise of humans might lurk on the island. The clouds edged across the face of the moon and blotted out the stars. Complete darkness fell on me and I stood there shivering until the sweet light returned with my courage. My trembling stopped, though my legs were shaky as I crept forward. Now I was near enough to identify it.

My chest shuddered in a great sigh of relief as I saw that it was Wadawaka. He did not want to be disturbed, for if he had there was cause enough from the commotion continuing behind me. He paid it no heed and stood there, a solitary figure immersed in himself. One hand was thrust beneath his jacket busily scratching away at the lice bites, then it slowed as a sound caught his ear. He cocked his dreadlocked head. His face moved from right to left as if he was tracking something; I could see nothing, the moonlight being too deceptive and hiding what he might be seeing from his position. Now he was staring down at the surface of the pool. It gleamed softly and the paperbark trees surrounding it made a slivering dry sound, though it had been raining. The branches swayed gently in a cold breeze. There was a soft plop and the flash of silver as a fish leaped up.

I wanted to go to my friend, but felt unable to move. I could only watch as he began to strip off his rough clothing as if breaking free of the strands of the spirit catcher that bound him. Now black and naked as the day he was thrust forth, he stood stretching, seeking to bring some energy back into his body. He shook himself, then zombie-like waded into the pool. When the water grew too deep, he floated, then swam. He neared the middle of the pool and it happened. I cried out as something with dark wings swooped down upon him. He gave a shout that was abruptly cut off as his head disappeared beneath the waves. The thing shrieked and its strange pitiful cries swept into my brain to release my body. I crept towards the bank. The thing circled screaming over the place where my friend had disappeared. Suddenly, it rose and flickered over me. A voice touched me like a soft caress as it darted away.

I knew what it was and why it was there. How could I not know when I recognised that voice and knew the mind behind it. I gave a shudder of remembered passion as I rushed to the pool edge where Wadawaka's pathetic pile of grubby clothing lay. I looked down at them. Had I imagined everything? Had he merely ducked beneath the water to grab up some bottom mud to scrub at his body? I thought about how filthy and vermin infested the schooner had become and my flesh crawled. I began pulling off my clothing to swim. But where was he? Wildly, I stared at the spot where the water bubbled and swirled about. Ripples spread out to hit the bank with a constant shook-shook like the shrouds of dead men flapping under the wind.

'Where are you, Wadawaka!' I shouted again and again. No answer. Had he become snagged on a dead tree resting beneath the water? Hurriedly, I pulled off the rest of my clothing and was ready to go after him. Then a hand touched my shoulder. I leapt about a metre into the air and came down in a crouch, my hand groping for the pistol I had thrust into my pile of clothes. Better ready than dead was my motto, and I was coming up, cocking it when there was a 'heh-heh-heh'. I knew that cackle too well. I uncocked the pistol and flung it back on top of my clothes, then turned to the old black man, white-bearded and with his grey hair braided into locks which were smeared with a darkness I knew was red ochre.

'Thank the ancestors,' I could not help exclaiming, to which he remarked,

'You're a silly fellow to allow someone to creep up on you like that.'

My black supposed father in those days had had the habit of putting me in my place and too often making me appear foolish. This was one of those occasions and I could only stand there and feel it. 'Been seeing over the island,' he said, thus explaining his absence from the camp. 'Lotta noise back there,' he added, with a jerk of his beard in that direction. 'Someone should see about it,' he observed, and was turning away from me, when I whispered with an intensity that made my words hiss out. 'Wadawaka, something terrible has happened to him. He's gone. Drowned!'

'Yeah, that thing's caught up with us and ... look,' he exclaimed, 'there he goes!'

There was a flurry in the centre of the pool and a magnificent animal, gleaming dark and light in the moonlight, suddenly broke the water and sped off into the night sky. Jangamuttuk stared after him, scratching his beard. 'I thought he was stronger,' he said. 'She got into his mind and now he's off without a word to us. Well, he won't find refuge with a thing like that. He'll learn sooner or later, but we can't hang around waiting for him to come to his senses. Someone'll have to go after him, I suppose. Now, just look at him. A fine sight, like an old goanna or a snivelling dog.'

'Oh, I don't know about that,' I exclaimed hotly, feeling that he was having a dig at my friend.

'Well, leave it be. Now what is all that crying and wailing from the camp?'

Was it the long voyage with its howling winds; was it that female thing that had taken on herself to make us her prey; or was it this island where we had just murdered an ugly ghost that afflicted our minds and even our ways of treating one another? My father had grown irritable and bitter; Wadawaka had suddenly decided to dash off alone, and as for my mother, Ludjee, well she was my mother. Now what could I say to put these inchoate feelings into words? I found that I could not and all that I could do was tell my father, who was also the spiritual adviser and healer of our mob, the sad story of how Hercules had cleft the head of the ghost in twain. As I spoke to him, in my mind I could see the splitting of the possum cap and the two glittering eyes falling apart into simple reddish stones as they tumbled into the fire. I told him how the skull had shattered and bits of bone and brain had splattered me. I described how the glittering blue eye of the ghost had burst with a plop so that he was truly as blind as he was dead, then how the blood had spurted up, dark and mysterious in the firelight and that I had tasted it and found it flavoured with the tart taste of rum and iron.

'You think too much of the effects rather than the causes,' my father replied in that soft voice he had been using since our poolside meeting, seeming to evade the intensity of my words. Instead he concentrated on the foul murder and the resulting blood vengeance, for the debt resulting from spilt blood had to be settled. He said that Hercules had committed a crime, no matter the cause, and it would bring a curse on us. 'I once thought,' he went on, again in that soft voice, 'that we were different from the ghosts, that we would not think of doing the things they did so casually. Now we have murdered and what shall this crime bring upon us, but hardship and suffering. We shall have to bear it, for Wadawaka must be rescued if we are to continue our voyage. Now purify yourself for you stink of blood and brain, while I check up on how that African is faring.'

Now my father, the shaman of our people, sat cross-legged. His chin fell upon his chest as he sank into himself, then his spine suddenly stiffened and all his bones cracked as he left his body and me. There wasn't anything else to do until he returned, but follow his words and bathe. I waded into the pool trying not to cringe at the thought of what might lurk beneath the surface. The night was cold, the water warm (even hot when I tried to touch the bottom), and there was a funny smell from it like that from a musket when fired. Still, I began to enjoy my bath, rubbing the bottom mud over me to rid myself of the pollution. Clean at last, I emerged to my dirty clothes. I tried to shake and wipe some of the bone and brain from them, but it was impossible and, unable to bear the touch of them, I decided to remain naked. It was nice to feel my skin crinkle under the cold, then break into goose bumps as my body adjusted its temperature.

I was just standing there feeling these sensations when my father returned from his psychic trip to tell me that Wadawaka had been well and truly caught by the balls, if not the cock, by the awful moma we had encountered before. He declared that he had to be rescued from her clutches and that our ancestors had given him a plan. 'It will be up to you,' he said with a smile. 'As Dingo you will snuff out his trail and find him. It's about time too, that you learnt how to take care of yourself in this country, both over and under her. You're the last of our young 'uns and after you, our race will be at an end. You must stay alive as long as you can and so you must pass those tests by which you go beyond being a mere man to that of a shaman. Getting cut was nothing compared to what you will have to endure, and when you first shape-changed, well, that might have been horrific; but the next stage is far worse.'

'But, but,' I protested, 'how am I to scent out Wadawaka when he flew off through the air? He's a leopard and much stronger than me. If he can be enthralled and captured, what might happen to me?'

'Dingo has a keen nose and can sniff out the track,' he answered simply.

'But if I go as Dingo, I will not be able to wear clothes or carry a weapon. If I turn back into a human, I will be defenseless as well as helpless unless, of course, my route is only on this island which is small enough for me to handle.'

'It isn't, but on that which lies spread out beyond this mud patch. There learn how to live on what the land provides. Fashion a spear, use firesticks to make a fire. Then as for clothing, you were born naked and stand now as nature made you. Raised by ghosts, you caught their habits and now you must forget them and survive, remember them and you die!'

With this he turned and walked towards the camp where the wailing had continued on intermittently. I turned and followed him. If I had to go naked, well, that was all right. What I didn't like was that survive or die thing.

The fires were glowing with masses of coals. No-one had added logs since the catastrophe. My aunties were cradling the body of Malone and wailing. My mother was trying to comfort them, while the men stared at the body with wide eyes and the other women now and again broke out into frenzied weeping. My father stopped in front of me and gestured without turning that I build up the fires. He walked to the central one on which I flung an armful of wood. As it blazed up, he raised a hand and said in a low voice that reached out to every ear. 'When we began this voyage there were things we thought we would never do. One of these was killing without remorse, for blood vengeance comes down on those who kill without pity. Well, there has been a murder this night and guilt has swooped down upon us. Our captain, our chief mate is gone and it is because of this crime. It must be atoned for, else our journey is doomed. The first thing is to purify this place. Ludjee and you other women, help those two take away the body. You men take off the canvas from the framework, then pile the sticks on the body. Make sure that it is covered completely.'

He stood there quietly until his orders were carried out. The wailing stopped and was replaced by sobs. Now as the eastern sky was lightening, Jangamuttuk flung the murder weapon into the pile of sticks which covered the body, then scattered the three fires over the ground and pyre. It caught and blazed up. 'Now collect our things and let us leave this place,' he said, then turned to stare at the hut. 'That ghost place too must be destroyed. Don't go inside, fling burning sticks through the doorway.'

By the time the hut was blazing, day was upon us and with the coming of light, our mood of gloom lightened enough for Jangamuttuk to send the men hunting while he, I and the women went around the island. Nadjee and Lorimee were still too distraught to help us, and they were left behind to continue their vigil at the remains of the pyre. As we left they were smearing the ashes over their faces. Later, I knew, they would cut off their hair to begin their period of official mourning.

We went across the tail of the island and then east to where the tail fattened out into the body of the lizard. There, I saw that the sea had scooped out a hollow in the island. It was a natural basin and if the water was deep enough could hold our schooner; I was worried about her falling into the wrong hands and leaving us stranded. Malone had said that others came to the island and if they arrived to find our deserted schooner anchored below Malone's old place, then what was there to prevent them from taking it? It had to be moved and this was an ideal place, being on the opposite shore to where we were now anchored and lying between mainland and island, it was sheltered from any storm which might arise. I went down to the shore and made my way to the entrance. The water there looked deep enough to hold our vessel; but I would have to make sure by taking a sounding from the dingy. I went back to our landing place and Nadjee and Lorimee flung up their doleful ashen faces at my arrival. They had the look of corpses about them; but at least they weren't wailing. I got them to row our boat around to the basin.

'You get used to anyone you live with,' Nadjee said in explanation for their mourning of a ghost who had owned them.

'Even though he made us do things we didn't want to,' Lorimee added.

'And unlike them others, he hardly ever hit us. In fact we hit him ...'

'He was good to us and only made us work.'

'What will we do without him,' they both wailed, rocking the boat and making me apprehensive that they would capsize it.

I was too young then to understand women and their relationships. I thought that they would consider themselves happy to be free of Malone and overjoyed at being reunited with their sister. But they missed their ghost and began talking about him and his odd habits, such as his penchant for being tied up and given a switching as long as the switch flipped out to sting his flesh, rather than to fall as a heavy blow. I listened, hardly able to make much of this conversation, and it did have an effect on them for they began laughing, saying that he had not been such a bad old egg. Cheered up by their conversation, they fell with a will to the rowing and soon we were passing through the narrow length of passageway that led into the basin proper. I took soundings as my friend had taught me. There was water enough in the channel and on the western side of the basin, though from the struggle we had to enter it, as the tide was on the ebb, there might be trouble getting in. I decided to try to get the schooner through when the tide was completely out and if this was impossible, then wait until it was on the rise. I checked the strait between island and mainland for an anchorage to use if we did have to wait and Nadjee pointed to the west where a line of water foamed. 'That's where you get across to the mainland,' she informed me. I nodded, that would have to be avoided.

'Rocky causeway and the mob over there used to cross, that is until Malone came,' Lorimee said.

'When he got drunk, he used to take potshots at them,' Nadjee added.

'And those mates of his, they went after the women.'

'Could never go there, cause of them being all stirred up. Get speared if we did.'

This caused me alarm, especially as they mentioned one of the mainland mob, who really had it in for them. How could I make my way through their land to find Wadawaka when they were on the warpath? I didn't fancy my chances if they caught a glimpse of me, and even less if I was captured. Well, Father was our spiritual leader and would have to work out a peace with them. They had to be pacified if I was to go over their land as either a dingo or human.

When we landed, seeing the smouldering hut set the women off again. They rushed to the remains of the pyre while I joined the men waiting for the fat kangaroos they had speared to finish cooking. I got four of them to man the boat and another two to get onto the schooner with me. With some difficulty we towed her around the coast and even with the tide at its lowest, we got her through the channel and anchored close to the western bank. As the sun was still quite high in the sky and the clouds were just bulky threats on the western horizon, we then rowed to where the rocky path stretched between island and mainland. It made access to the island easy and lay open for anyone to use.

We arrived back when the kangaroos were being pulled out of the earth oven and I immediately went to my father to tell him about moving the vessel. He was supervising the shaving of the heads of his wife's sisters and merely grunted. I told him about the causeway and was turning away when he said: 'That is where we will camp.'

'There?' I blurted. 'Is it safe?'

'Safe enough while you go off after Wadawaka,' he retorted, then laughed and said: 'Dingoes are not known for their bravery, but for their cunning; though when their backs are against the wall, they are known to fight the good fight. We shall camp there because it is from there that you shall begin your quest. Across the causeway is an old ceremonial ground which is a centre of power. I must conduct our ceremony of purification there during which you shall be expelled as a scapegoat; but don't worry we shall be friends with the local mob by then.'

'If we're not,' Hercules, who had been listening, cut in, 'and they cause us trouble, I'll give them trouble,' and he lifted his heavy club and slammed it onto the ground.

Jangamuttuk stared at him and knitted his brow as he replied: 'Last night was your work and for it we are suffering the consequences. The guilt must be expiated not compounded with more innocent blood.'

'I wasn't talking about blood,' Hercules remonstrated, 'I was talking about just a tap or two on the head to bring them to their senses.'

'Yes and was it just a tap you gave that ghost,' Jangamuttuk retorted. 'It cost us Wadawaka and if we do not find him, that will be the end of our voyage west.'

'What about this boy,' Hercules replied with a glance at me. 'He's his friend and knows how to handle this big canoe. And see that, that is the sun setting. Just aim at it and you are heading west. So, no problems!'

'No, no,' Jangamuttuk groaned, 'we need a rest from that schooner. My stomach shifts when I think of being on her. I want the solid ground under my feet for a while and so do you. Your vomit really stinks, you know. We bide a bit here, for this boy is to undergo an ordeal by which he might become a shaman. He'll go after Wadawaka, while you and I, we shall sing and dance with the local mob, eh? Now is that the sweet smell of kangaroo ready and waiting for our mouths. Let us eat and then shift our camp.'

CHAPTER FOUR

'I am Jangamuttuk, Master of the Ghost Dreaming,' my father and our shaman declared to whatever inimical sentient forces might be within earshot, striking his clapsticks vigorously to underline his words as he led us in procession across the causeway.

I was surrounded by the women who performed as if they were at a real funeral service. They were in a way – mine; for as a scapegoat I was to be driven forth and be as one dead to my mob. 'Kyee, kyee,' they wailed and one of them, was it my mother, Ludjee, or perhaps one of her sisters, who were in mourning for the ghost and now had their heads denuded of hair and glistening with charcoal and fat, began slapping her stomach in a monotonous sodden rhythm. They surrounded me protectively and I felt that I needed to hide among them and perhaps escape my fate. I was cold too, for since the dip in the lake I had gone naked and for this ceremony my father had simply rubbed grey ash all over my body. Now, I really looked like an ambulating corpse and cold as one too. The rest of my mob, except for Jangamuttuk and my aunties in mourning, were warm in their fur capes. Well, at least I was going on a quest and they weren't. Still that was one of the things which was sending a chill through me. Who knew what would happen and one thing I did and did not want to happen, was to meet my mistress and feel her hand on me. I shivered and it wasn't because of the cold. I glanced down to where I was getting an erection. How embarrassing it would be for a corpse to have this thing sticking out in front of him, but I knew how to make it limp. I thought of the horror of that mistress. The dread arose as my penis not only dropped, but shrunk. Now, I didn't want to think about her, and tried to push away the figure of that strange white female phantom that beckoned me. She called me to her, but I had to remain with my father. I had to go through the whole ceremony or else I was lost.

'I, the singer of songs will open the gates of the underground,' my father intoned, stopping at the foot of the causeway as if there was a physical barrier there.

Crack, crack went his clapsticks, opening the way and driving back the presence I had felt before.

'The passageway gapes wide,' chorused the men.

'Kyee, kyee,' wailed the women pressing themselves against me so that I felt the needed warmth of their bodies. It was then that the men descended on them. They were thrust aside and I was stolen from their midst.

'Kyee, kyee,' they cried, 'the womb gapes wide.'

'He will descend below,' Jangamuttuk chanted.

'Through that way gaping for him,' the men chorused.

I shivered for I knew that I was to be driven from their midst.

Now Hercules clasped one of my arms and thrust me away from the others. In front of my father who dolefully clapped his sticks, I stepped onto the causeway of stone linking the island to the mainland. The men gave a shout and the women shrieked louder than ever as I walked between the waves which had receded to reveal the thin path of stone which in places was just piles of pebbles through which the salt water rose to splash my feet. The water was colder than the air. My skin raised goose bumps to stop the heat from leaving my body.

Now the solidity and hopefully the warmth of the mainland was before me. Soon I would be loping across its vast flatness and this should have roused my doggy instincts, except that these were submerged within the human, George, who now stumbled from the causeway where it petered out in the sand. Under instructions from my father, I walked to the left, diagonally away from the ocean and towards two spikes of rocky pillars. This was supposedly where the boro ground was. Behind me the others came with my father at their head. It must have been an amusing sight to have seen them following a youth covered all over with white ash, resembling a corpse. Perhaps it was, but the local mob were not amused by our antics. Suddenly, a spear hissed past and whacked into the ground behind me. I was about to look back, when the blackfellows, naked except for their pubic coverings and covered all over in red ochre and white pipeclay, emerged from between the two tall pillars of rock to confront us with pointing spears.

They were led by a giant of a man who was bald by nature rather than ritual design. His round dome of a head was daubed over with ochre then divided into sections by white painted lines. It looked funny, though none of us were in the mood for laughing as they held their spears ready to cast. Bald Head scowled even more and then began furiously biting at his huge black beard. He jerked out a hand for his fellows to spread out in a spaced line before our now stationary and bunched mob. I was all by myself between the two mobs and I expected a spear to pierce me through any minute. My toes curled into the sand as the big man strode towards me. I breathed a sigh of relief as he went past me as if I did not exist to confront my father. I turned and watched as he stopped, spreading his legs apart and tightening his buttock muscles. He was a regular tight arse, I thought, as he began shouting. 'You look like blackfellows, but who cares! This is not your land. Get off it now. You're not wanted here. That island is taboo and only evil comes from it, so get back where you belong!'

'That may be,' Jangamuttuk said quietly, 'but then aren't there men who can combat evil and drive it away. These are called shamans, you know, and as for that island, a ghost lived there and he has been burnt up. Also, where he lived has been smoked and purified. Now we have come across that narrow path of stone to do ceremony. Let us pass!'

'No, and if you want to know, that island was taboo long before the ghost arrived,' the big blackfellow retorted, tugging again at his bush of a beard, then fingering what seemed to be a kangaroo bone pushed through the septum of his bulbous nose. The rest of his mob affected the same ornamentation and in less distressing circumstances, this might have had us rolling around in stitches; but we were too scared for that and simply stared back at them as they stared at us, as he glared at us, even flinging an angry look over his shoulders as if he wanted to challenge me. Although I could see only his back and a bit of his side, the tensing and relaxing of muscles clearly revealed what his more expressive front was doing. He sneered at my mob's fur cloaks, slapped his own bare but hairy chest as if it meant something, for although it was chilly it was nowhere cold enough to freeze your balls off, then shouted: 'I am Yarikulli, Strongarm! I am boss of this mob and this country. No-one can walk here without my permission. You are unwelcome, go!'

He shook his fist at the island as if it was now ours and declared: 'If you indeed have killed the ghost there, then you are welcome to it. Have it, and if there is no more disappearing of women, children and even men, if this does not continue, then you may come back and perform your ceremonies. There,' he turned around and looked past me to his mob, 'that should take care of that.'

'Well, perhaps we don't like bony noses,' Hercules jerked out in a sudden shout. 'We are guests and as such accept the weird appearances of our hosts. So thank you for your hospitality. Go gnaw on your bones.'

'And,' Jangamuttuk broke in, 'as shaman and healer of this mob I declare that if there is evil I shall dispel it. I am Jangamuttuk, Master of the Ghost Dreaming, and well able to do this. Before, together with Waai, the shaman of the mob to the east of you, we rid that land of a thing which walked in the night and drank blood. Yes, I am well able to do such work.'

'And so did our one, mate, until we got rid of him. Get back to your island. We want none of your tricks here. Yes, we had Milyado, Bandicoot. What did he do, but snuffle about all day for food. We drove him from us so that he could go into the wilderness and learn more tricks to beguile us. We have our weapons and these are enough. We don't need religion to muddle things.'

'Yet, you still speak of an evil. Is it as solid as the shafts of your spears? Have you been able to spear that which cannot be speared?' Jangamuttuk almost chanted, putting himself into a dance stance, striking his sticks and then indeed chanting: 'Before us is the outcast, we send him to his death.'

'Yes, I am ready to talk of death, for lately there was that of my brother,' Strongarm said, raising his weapon in his right hand and gesturing with his left for his mob to lift theirs. Without enthusiasm, they did so. In fact, standing behind him I could see from the slackness of his muscles that Strongarm was losing his enthusiasm for confrontation. I thought that if he continued his pretense, our own strongman, Hercules, would detect his weakness and rush in to enjoy himself.

'We are here conducting a funeral service, which in all the lands I have visited, has been respected,' Jangamuttuk said with a great sigh. He in turn tugged at his beard, before he added: 'And in all those lands, there are ceremonies of welcome. All the mobs without exception have one and you are the first lot to have none. This I find strange indeed.'

'Do you take us for savages,' retorted the giant, tossing away his spear disdainfully. 'Of course we have one, but it will not be to your liking. Everyone who wishes to be a guest on our land, must fight me. If you prevail you may stay, if not go! Choose a weapon,' he shouted at Jangamuttuk. It would have been no contest as my father was old and had lately suffered from seasickness.

Jangamuttuk was about to reply when Hercules with an exaggerated look of ferocity hefted his club and got in first. 'Well, that is easily done,' he exclaimed, striding forward and bringing it crashing down on Strongarm's head.

The man tottered, appeared to recover, then slid to the earth unconscious.

'Wish other mobs had such a ceremony,' shouted our strongman in glee. 'That wasn't much of a fight. Come on, I'll take you all on. Come on, I like this ceremony of welcome.'

He strode towards the mob of local blackfellows who quickly backed away, their eyes on the upraised waddy. It was then that an older man stepped out from them. He spread his hands open to show that he held no weapon before beginning to speak: 'That Strongarm needed to be shown that his methods are those of a bully. He invented this silly custom and you have shown him this day that he can be beaten. Welcome to a sad land where blows fail to help us. Something prowls here, taking our women and children, and occasionally a man.'

'Something?' replied my father. 'Well, maybe it was that ghost on the island. He with others like him stole the two sisters of my wife. They were with him when we came to the island and he unfortunately met with an accident which has laid on us a blood debt. I must remove it before we go on, for we are fleeing to the west which hopefully is free of the infestation which has struck our land. We know of ghosts and their ways. They carried off women and children and if the men sought to prevent them, they were killed. They harried us until we stole one of their boats and escaped. Strongarm should have used his physical strength and left Milyado to handle any psychical aspects that is the province of a shaman. Still, what has not been done, has not been done. I am the Master of the Ghost Dreaming and have ceremonies which will remove any evil influences. In fact we are on your land to conduct a ceremony in conjunction with this boy here,' he added, indicating me with a pouting of his lips. 'He is on a quest and after we send him on his way, I will conduct a Moma ceremony to help you. But to do this, I need to use your ceremonial ground.'

'Well, there is no problem in that,' the man replied and then both of then stopped and regarded Strongarm who was recovering consciousness. He got up on one elbow and glowered at Hercules, then at Jangamuttuk: 'I was not ready,' he muttered. 'If I had been, he would be the one lying here.'

A huge bellow from Hercules made him fall back on the ground.

'You were felled with a single blow,' the spokesman of his mob said with a shrug. 'While you were asleep these strangers, now our guests, have offered to help us. They ask only for the use of a ceremonial ground.'

'Help us, help us, we shall see, see,' Strongarm muttered, rubbing his head, then groggily getting to his feet and attempting to glare through his pain. 'Well, they may conduct a ceremony; but I will remain on my guard. I do not trust them. Well, let them do their ceremony. It will entertain us and we will even participate in the fun. See those two pillars of rock. We call them the Sisters. They mark the edge of the taboo land. Once they were witches which our strongman, my ancestor, vanquished. Their bodies then became those rocks and their spirits went to the island where they continue to lurk. Well, be that as it may. In the space between the rocks there is a boro ground where our shaman used to hold ceremonies to pacify the evil about us, but he failed to do so, and we drove him away from our camp.'

'You chased him away,' the man who had spoken before retorted.

'Everyone, but you, knows that it is necessary to have a shaman for spiritual health. With him things might have remained bad, but with him gone, things are worse.'

'Well, he was a trickster without power,' shouted back Strongarm, 'and this one will prove just like him!'

'You shall see the extent of my powers just as you have seen the extent of Hercules' powers,' Jangamuttuk replied softly. 'I have been given this new ceremony which has come down from the north. It is to remove evil from the land. It is said that there is this devil, a moma, which roams around freely doing harm. She must be snared and tied with psychic bonds so that she can do no harm. This is what my ceremony does. Perhaps your shaman did not know of it, though if you had not exiled him, I might have passed it on to him. It must be received in the proper manner. Anyway, that is besides the point and I will perform it. This is only proper, for it is said a guest with empty hands is as welcome as a poisonous snake in one's hut. And speaking of huts, where do you wish us to camp?'

'Right where you are,' stated Strongarm. 'And if you don't like it, then go back to your island.'

'Thank you. This is the best place for us. It is near, but not too close to the boro ground.'

'Well, beggars can't be choosers, especially when their only weapon is their sarcasm,' Strongarm snarled. 'Be as you say you are and after the ceremony you might get to camp next to us.'

'But this is what we need,' Jangamuttuk insisted. 'Now let us see the boro ground. Soon it will be dark and it is then that we begin our ceremony.'

And so it was to be, and best of all I was not to be driven out then, though perhaps later. At the time I did not know and was as excited as the rest of them when we collected at the foot of the two pillars of stone towering over the ceremonial ground. Against one of them a hut had been constructed with a roof of leafy branches. Sheets of bark made the walls and a doorway faced the circular boro ground. A fire blazed in front of it and others glowed near the other pillar. The women sat surrounding me either protectively or to keep me from running away. The men sat near them and I felt that they were also keeping an eye on me. The local blackfellows clustered about Strongarm at the other pillar. I looked towards them and saw that Hercules had had the audacity to sit with the strangers, then I saw why. He held a pair of clapsticks as did some of the other men. He was to set the rhythm for them. He did so, crack crack-crack, and the others took it up.

Apprehension grew within me as my father emerged from the shelter. Two long bands of red were painted across his forehead, down both sides of his face, his neck and body to end on his thighs. He wore bark amulets in which had been fastened short bits of rag. A longer and wider piece was wrapped about his head so that his hair stood up in a tuft. He wore ghost trousers, over which he had placed his pearl shell pubic covering. Now he lifted each leg in turn and singed the leggings covering the bottoms of the trousers over the fire in front of the shelter. As he stepped away from the fire, I saw that the red bands gleamed with a phosphorescent greenish glow. There was also an eye shape glowing from the centre of his forehead. He now turned to the doorway of the hut and reached inside. He pulled out a short forked stick on the ends of which had been attached sharpened kangaroo femur bones. He gestured at the three audience groups in turn. Under Hercules' direction, the men with the clapsticks now began a slow rhythm. The women around me started clapping their hands in the vee of their thighs to create a deep sombre sound which made my heart thud in unison.

'Pilil aroola wotya rum brina,' sang Jangamuttuk.

'Pilil aroola wotya rum brina,' repeated our mob, while the women shrilly screamed, 'Kyee, kyee,' and set my ears to buzzing.

Now, in a marching step, my father stamped about the circle, stopping in front of both groups of men and pointing with his stick, threatening them and challenging them to take part in the dance. Some of our mob got up and so did a number of the local blackfellows, though they did not know the dance. Still, they added their own steps and kept to the rhythm as best they could.

Hercules struck up a furious clacking rhythm which was followed by the other clapstick players. The dancers stamped along to the staccato beat. From the scowling darkness came a whirling sound which rose higher and higher into a shrill shriek that shredded my nerves. I began to feel really scared as the women's voices rose along with it. 'Kyee, kyee,' they screamed, thudding their hands into the vee of their thighs so forcefully that their bodies rocked against me. The noise raced up to a crescendo and they suddenly ejected me from their midst and out towards the dancing men. I stumbled rather than danced forward and the men fell back. I stood there absurdly covered in the grey ash. I felt embarrassed and a figure of ridicule rather than some apparition returned from the grave. My father then gestured and I understood that I was to dance. I raised and stamped my legs half-heartedly. My father came towards me jerking the two-pronged wand towards me. Now he was in range to jab it viciously at me. I backed away and he kept on jabbing, forcing me to the edge of the ground. The men now dashed to the fires, snatched up blazing brands and flung them at me. The women wailed, then watched in a silent huddle. Now all the dancers made a concerted rush at me, waving smoking sticks. I turned and fled from the clearing. The sticks rained after me and some started fires that tore away the concealing darkness. A double-pronged wand flashed towards my chest and with a cry I sprang into the blackness at the base of the rocky pillar. There, I turned into Dingo and loped away followed by shouts from my mob. I had been cast out and also I had begun my quest. If I failed, I could not return. My doggy mind tried to grasp this, but gave up as the interesting smells of the bush overpowered it. Then came her voice calling me to come to her.

CHAPTER FIVE

How different I felt, as harsh and unforgiving as the land. I raised my snout and stared along it, then widened my field of vision to take in the landscape directly in front of me, then extending on both sides to almost three quarters of a circle. It was like one of those panoramas you have. Then there came to me the slightly musty scent of a bandicoot and I snuffled it up and followed it into a niche notched into the steep escarpment wall. I trotted forward, noticing how on both sides towered rocky cliff faces, the edge of the interior plateau. I was not apprehensive because there were plenty of fallen boulders to hide among if danger threatened. And it might, for the feeble flicker of a campfire came from around a bend to make me wary. I crouched, but the strong smell of that fleshy bandicoot made me slaver and forget myself. I crept forward and came to the edge of the fire. There was no bandicoot, only a bent-over human figure moving slowly about close to the ground and from him came the powerful scent as if he had recently gorged himself on the animal. I settled myself on my haunches and searched about for scraps. I couldn't find any. I continued to sit there letting my mind fill with the scene before me.

First, there came the indistinct mutterings, too slurred to be deciphered. The human felt about, found pieces of wood and flung them onto the fire which now blazed up to reveal that the figure was an old blind man, stringy and hard. Finally, he stopped his groping and tossing of pieces of wood and huddled close to the blaze, warming himself against the cold of the night. It was then that I crept into the firelight and lay down across from him. He was a sightless thing with weak organs of sound and taste and so of little threat. I lay close to the fire and luxuriated in the warmth while the ancient human muttered on.

'Blind eyes do not need any light. Darkness is enough, but old bones need this to keep off the cold, just as my skin needs a kangaroo skin. Now where is it? Eyes are well enough, but there's other senses as well. I can smell it out, by golly', and he got on his hands and knees and sniffed vigorously. I tensed, feeling that I was about to be discovered for I was lying on his kangaroo skin, but when his nose stopped its twitching, and pointed outside the circle of light, I relaxed again.

'Something's out there, eh? Well, I've got something for that something.' He felt around and took up a spear in his shaking hand. 'I'll get him this time. He'll feel the strength of my wooden point, hardest wood you can get and if it doesn't work, I'll pressure a stone point and that'll get him for sure. Yeah get him, though if I do, what with the stink and all those crows fluttering about, I'll have to shift camp. Don't want to do that. This place and I agree and the walls keep out the cold wind, well when it's not blowing directly from the south, and then if I move, well, where will it be to. Back to the camp, I guess Strongarm's forgotten me by now. Well, even if he has, I'm not going back there. No, feel safer here. This spot knows me and I know it. So I'll forget the spear and keep close to the fire. Who'll want an old man like me, with blood thin as water in his veins ...'

Then I almost shat myself as I found eyes staring from the dark, close to the ground and reflecting the flame of the fire, focused on the old man. If he had still had his sight, he too would have seen them and the low squat body that was a blacker part of the dark, then he too would have been petrified with fright. I was just about to slink away when the eyes rose to the height of a human, who now stepped boldly into the firelight, glanced at me, then stopped beside the muttering old man.

He quavered along in his monotone. It was quite lulling in a way and I knew that as long as it continued my father, for that was who the human was, would not start carrying on about me being a slacker for not getting on with my quest. Well, let him scold. I was happy to have him keeping an eye on me; it was his duty as a father to see that I came to no harm, either in my human or dog shape. It had hurt, too, to be expelled from my mob without a by your leave. Well, at least that had been put to rights with him sitting across from me listening to the same silly old bugger going on and on.

'Knew there was someone, or something there. Smelt like a dog, then a goanna, now a man. Bloody bush, filled with all these critters who come and plague me. Give me a good old spirit any day, rather than one of these so-called Dreaming animals. Some Dreaming, eh? Well, I've got me own animal, same as a lot of other blokes and women. That's why I got a sharp nose and can smell out the blood lust many walks away. One ghost down, how many to go? Got a sharp nose. You know blood calls for blood and the parting of the ways. Smell it here; nothing to do with me, but can smell it. What's that? Who are you? Answer, I hear and smell you. Heard that thud when you landed. Not a tree around, so did you leap from the cliff? Tall jump, but you might've clambered down. Goanna or man, what are you? What about that dog? Run down a sheer cliff face, did he?'

Well, at last my father and shaman of our mob gave a deep sigh as the monologue finally got to him. He broke with the flow, to speak. 'Well, we old fellows feel the cold, especially when we are without any covering,' he said politely. 'Need to sit at your fire and warm myself. I am Jangamuttuk, Master of the Ghost Dreaming, and a guest in your country; but why are you away from your mob and all by yourself? You should have a woman or two to look after you!'

'A woman or two or three, eh? Well, I had them and was content, till that Strongarm got above himself and blamed me for bringing that evil on our land that blinded me and aged me overnight. He blamed me for what was happening even though I was the first victim. What could I do but use what powers I had even though they lacked the necessary energy. I tried performing ceremonies, but how could I concentrate when all I was hearing was the sneering of that Strongarm who finally, after getting over his fear of me, drove me out. Tells me to go commune with the spirits and get some power before I showed my face again. Even told me to get some eyes, the bastard! Strongarm, more likely Bonehead! But what can an old fellow do, when his sight's gone along with whatever power he once had. Well, the women come and give me food, bless their hearts, but they have to come in a mob now because there is that thing stalking our land. Got to get power to combat that. Spirits! Well, there's spirits all right, spirits here, a spirit there, some sort of devil over there, maybe two or three and they come to me, and you know what? The buggers laugh at me. Did you ever hear a spirit laugh? It's a high and long keening like a happy curlew's cry, as if she had just found her babies after they had been stolen from her. Well, enough of that, who might you be? Or what are you for that matter? Your smell's pretty powerful you know and I've got a nose for such things.'

'Well, I know who you are. I've just come from your mob and have heard about you. That old bloke who's not much good with the magic. Old fellow by the name of Milyado. Bandicoot, eh? Well, is it true that you don't need eyes, but have ears that can hear the wind rising far across the ocean, with a nose that can smell the rain falling far to the east and west, and claws that have dug many a chasm? Better than a silly young dog, eh?' my father replied, finishing off with a dig at me.

'Hear you, don't I? But you know what, they keep on plaguing me.'

'Well, old shaman and spiritual brother, Bandicoot, use your powers to drive whatever it is away. Become your Dreaming animal, regurgitate your crystal weapon and dispel the gloom over this land.'

'Yeah, what crystal and what light to bring? I am as powerless as any of my mob, including that Strongarm. Claws and teeth are not as fast as my legs. See them coming, and off like a dingo. Was thinking of using this spear on the last one, but why? Kill it here and it stinks up the place. Want to stay here, you know. Cosy! And what's this about crystal? Look at this lack of teeth and talk to me about magic crystals. All I'm good for is throwing up the dirt. I can still dig a mean burrow.'

'Well, you should know about crystals. When you were initiated as a shaman ...'

'I'm so old I can't even remember that; but I've got only gums now and then even the claws are all worn down from the digging, but take a feel of this spear! Point sharp as that female thing's eye teeth. She nibbled at me once and I felt them. Just feel it! Now, that's sharp. Old Bandicoot's eyes mightn't be good anymore; but he doesn't need them when he's got the sun in the morning and the moon at night, except he can't see them and often he can't tell if its day or night – but forget all that, it's only a carry-on, he's got a secret, you know. If he wants to, he can see all right; but why should he when he likes the warm darkness. There's nothing like burrowing down into the soft warm earth or slashing your way through a hard hot one. Just imagine my front claws loosening the dirt and the hind legs pushing it behind me. I go down and down until I get tired and then curl up into a tight ball far from the light to dream on about what is far below where the stones glow. Yeah, but then there is that devil and he has taken over my best burrow, one that went down and down into the earth and came out onto that vast cavern. He's inclined to be argumentative too. He likes the night when he can flit as a shadowy thing, just a slither of dead bones being dragged in a sack towards some lair where they will be lovingly pawed over. He sounds like that, though sometimes there is also a gnawing as he goes by. I hear him, flapping, flapping along like a piece of bark against a tree, then like that piece of bark, he becomes detached and flutters off into the darkened sky. He's a bloodsucker, you know, but he doesn't care for bandicoot flesh or old man's blood.

You know he comes here to taunt me and to gloat. How the deadman's breath splutters in his rotting throat as he snarls out words. 'Shaman, I like them young and juicy and you are old and dry.' And there's another, no blackfellow in her way and behaviour. She titters and drifts about me as she tells me to rub myself. And I yell back, 'Get away you strange shrew,' and she laughs more shrilly and presses her body against mine. A body which is as cold as a corpse; but her breasts are soft and firm in that alluring way women's breasts are. Still, too cold for an old man like me and her mouth reeks of blood and spunk. She's a stealer of souls too, for she got at that other one and turned him. He was Strongarm's brother who went off one evening and returned the next a thing apart from us. I kept my eye on him and when he went after a woman and ripped at her throat, I flung my spear and he ran off dragging it like a wounded kangaroo. I followed closely; but I was too old for the chase and soon had to stop. I implored Strongarm to run him down, for as he was his brother, he would incur no blood guilt if he did so; but the bonehead only laughed and said that I should look after my women better, for the female he attacked was my favourite wife, Winniaree. He got her the next night thanks to that so-called boss of our mob who did nothing. They say blood's thicker and tastier than water and in his case I believe it. He protected the thing because it had been his younger brother and it still roams free.'

'Well, has that younger brother or the other thing been through here tonight?'

'There was a flapping and a whispering as he flew past. The whispering might have been the wind, but he circled my camp thrice, then went off towards the coast just as I got to thinking about getting this spear ready for his white heart. You know once he was a regular blackfellow, now he is as pale as a ghost. How he gleams in the moonlight as he flies by and the sight gets to you if you let it; but he needs to be destroyed, and that's what this spear's for. I had it well hidden and it took me an hour or two to find it. I have to get him through the heart to kill him; but then I got to thinking about how this spot'll be polluted and I'd have to move. No way! Let him haunt the nights. I've got a liking for this place. It's close to everything I need. Let him have my burrow. He's fouled that anyway. Still, it was a favourite one; but not the best. It led down and down, far down into the earth. My Bandicoot ancestor did the first digging and I was the guardian, keeping it open for our use. There's another not so far away, but Snake made that and I don't use it.'

'Well, old fellow,' my father broke in, as Milyado gulped down a breath and before he could go on. 'You should know these things: the underground and all that. You know the entrances, those which are safe for beings like me to use. I need to know about one of them.' He stared straight at me where I lay dozing and said: 'You see my son is supposed to be on a quest, one which will lead him deep into the earth.'

I gave a startled yelp; and the old bandicoot man instantly whispered: 'Hush, keep quiet, I heard a strange cry as if from a startled victim. Hush, the sound of leathern wings flapping this way. Pray that he isn't partial to goanna blood, though as you're almost as old as I am (I can smell the age on you), he will pass you up. He loves young things vibrant with strong blood.'

I was quaking at this, when my father declared: 'But will I pass him up! I intend to rid you of him and then you'll be able to use your favourite burrow and, in exchange, show me the passageway by which my son may descend. One follows the other,' he finished off, as the sound of the wings was almost directly overhead. He shimmered and where he had been sitting squatted a large goanna. He slivered his head about, his tongue licked out once, twice, then a third time. Now he held a glowing crystal in his mouth.

Suddenly a dark shape shifted across the sky, and he darted into the shadows while I, intent on watching the transformation of my father, stayed where I was, remaining as motionless as I could as, with a plop, a huge bat fell out of the sky. It fluttered on the ground for only an instant before it changed into a tall, powerful albino blackfellow who glared at the old bandicoot man with savage eyes and snarled: 'I've come to see you old fellow, tell you what happened to your last faithful wife. I'll sit by you and we'll discuss her attributes and how she tasted ... but what is this, a sweet young dingo.' He took a long stride towards me before he sensed another presence. He whirled and sprang towards the huge bulky shape-shadow which instantly lifted into the sky and, silhouetted against the night sky, showed as a giant goanna. Now it swooped down towards the albino blackfellow who at once twisted into the shape of the large white bat, unfolded his wings and darted up towards his attacker.

I breathed a sigh of relief, then gathering my courage sprang into the sky to help my father. There he was retreating from the bat, writhing in the effort to evade its lunges. Now, the bat came up under him, but as it did so, Goanna fell off to one side and dropped down towards the surface of the inland plateau. Not to be denied his prey, the flying mammal darted after him, steeply angling its descent to overtake him in the air. The bat was about to intersect his flight path when my father turned abruptly. The crystal in his mouth flashed and a red ray lanced out to strike his pursuer. The mammal's wings collapsed and it fluttered helplessly towards the earth. Goanna came after him, keeping his ray on the thing. The crystal glowed from red to white. A silent scream began and continued, until with a thud the bat hit the ground. Goanna landed beside him, while I stayed up in the sky in case the thing recovered and darted up or away.

It was injured, but still able to transform, changing back into the powerfully built blackfellow, but he seemed to have lost the use of his arms. They hung down, like dead sticks at his sides. Still, he snarled defiance and his legs were working, for he used them with good effort to put some distance between himself and Father. He made for the edge of the plateau, where a hole puffed up from the surface like a lanced boil, but Goanna leapt into the air and landed beside it. As his feet touched the ground, he changed into my father, Jangamuttuk, Master of the Ghost Dreaming, and calmly waited for the thing to reach him.

I looked down at where he stood and saw where floods had scarred the swelling and in places had piled up the trunks and branches of uprooted trees and shrubs. They lay there in battered broken masses as if the thrust of the waters had been more than terrific. Now my father picked up a branch with a jagged end. The injured albino staggered towards him with his mouth gaping. Where his eye-teeth should have been, were fangs which were longer and sharper than my own. With a scream of rage, then of anguish, the albino raised his evil face to the sky where the new day was dawning, and charged my father, who instantly flung the bough. There was an ungodly shriek as the jagged point hit his chest and pierced him through to the heart. I was in no doubt of this when the thing collapsed. Now my father bent over him and as I descended, I saw blood begin to gush from his mouth. Great dollops and strings of blood that made me almost want to go to him and place my mouth over his to catch the flood; but as I landed, the flow stopped, the thing shuddered and lay still.

'That's the end of him,' my father said to himself, ignoring me as if I were some invisible phantom. 'Though to make sure, I should cut off his head.'

He searched the ground and found a hard granite rock, then another. He examined them, then suddenly clapped them together. One of them broke along a minute fracture. The edge was sharp, but he was not quite satisfied until he had shaped it into a blade. He then went to where the creature lay and knelt beside him. He placed a stone under the nape of the neck so that the throat was revealed. Quickly my father struck at the throat with the stone blade. The skin parted and gaped. There was a further rush of blood. He waited a moment, then struck again and again until the head parted from the body and rolled away from the trunk. Its sightless eyes stared up at me and the elongated eye-teeth gleamed palely.

'Well, that's done,' Jangamuttuk said to himself.

He picked up the head by the hair which had been bound into a bun at the back of the head and then caked with clay so that it was rigid and hard like a short piece of blackboy tree. He swung it three times, then let go. It described an arc past me and landed on the edge of the hole.

'Perhaps old Bandicoot might want to see it,' he muttered to himself, having had second thoughts about disposing of the evil head.

There was a shimmer and Goanna appeared. He ambled over to the head, picked it up in his teeth, then took to the air, circling over the corpse before descending to land at the fire where Bandicoot still sat. I landed behind him and quietly took my place at the pile of coals. My father heaped it up a bit, then said: 'He won't trouble you any more.'

He picked up the head and placed it in the old fellow's hands. Bandicoot's fingers stroked the head and touched the fangs. He shuddered and exclaimed: 'I don't want that thing here. Wasn't much of a man was he to end up like that. That Strongarm thought otherwise though and even blamed me for doing this to him. Idiot, what did he take me for? Well, when you go, that goes with you, and while you're at it you might think of that other, that foreign female thing. With its mate gone, she might be even more deadly. Get rid of her, get rid of her, I don't want that female fluttering about me with her exquisite fingers plucking at me as if I belonged to her. No, I don't!'

'In time, in good time,' Jangamuttuk shrugged. 'I did not come here to kill blood suckers. Our friend and chief mate, Wadawaka has gone missing and my son George is looking for him. It's a wide land and he could keep on searching until he's as old and grey as you are; but then he has old Bandicoot to help him, hasn't he? That head with the fangs, it's a mite heavy for me to carry away. I need to be certain of a thing or two, before I cart it off. Bandicoots scuttle about in the oddest places and, merging with the greyness of the shadows, sniff out secrets. They know everything!'

'Well, maybe, maybe when the dark is on the earth and it becomes as blind as I am. It's then, Bandicoot, he goes out, keen sense of smell and all that. It makes him a magician of a sorts. But now I feel that the end of the darkness and the sun is there to put old Bandicoot to sleep. I'm not much use in the day, that I aren't. Still, anything to rid me of that head. You know there's this little ritual involving heads like that one. Just the thing to seek out that friend of yours. If you promise to leave me alone, I'll just do it. First, it needs to be stuck in the ground. You have to mount it on a short stake for me. Hammer one end into the ground and the other into the neck, right into the pipe so that it can swivel easily. Put it right in front of me, so that I can touch it, if need be, then after I've done, get rid of it instantly.'

My father followed Bandicoot's instructions and stuck a stake into the ground, then jammed the windpipe down on it. He pushed it about a few times so that it moved easily, then waited as Bandicoot muttered some words, then threw a couple of handfuls of ashes at the face. Much of it missed, but enough splattered to smear the dead unseeing eyeballs. Now, he muttered some more and the head shivered and began to rotate. It stopped as if it were staring at the escarpment, then shifted again coming to a final stop with the face downwards and towards the northwest.

'He'll be over there and as the face is looking down, underground.'

'As I knew and the entrance ...?'

'Now, not for a bandicoot, but say, for a human. Well, old Bandicoot knows them tunnels into the earth, that is those that were dug by his ancestors. Still, you don't want one of them, you need, say, one made by Snake. He's good at them, but not as good as we are. Now let me consider. What will be suitable? That sun is climbing the sky and making me very tired, sleepy. Wait until the night and I'll take you to the best. A large one, just like a hallway into the earth.'

'I can't wait that long. My mob and yours are at loggerheads. I should be there. What about that hole that looks like the earth has an abcess? I killed him as he was rushing to go down it. It's big enough for a boy or a dog to descend.'

'Oh, that one. Fouled by him, you know, but it goes right down underground, though there are things in it. Still, it'll do, now let me sleep.'

'You're coming along with me. It's not far, and the day is hardly upon us,' said Jangamuttuk.

'Do I have to?' complained the old man.

'Yes.'

'Right, if I must I must, just to get rid of you and the head of course.' With that, the old man changed into a bandicoot. He ran hither and thither sniffing, then raised his head and stared at the huge goanna. With an undulation that began at his snout and ended at the end of his rat tail, his grey body unfolded into the air and he darted off. Goanna lumbered after him and I followed.

Bandicoot set a straight course, though darting from this side to the other as if he were following a scent through the sky that only he could smell. I ambled in their wake feeling the growing pangs of hunger. I would have to hunt soon; but this was more important for the time being. We reached the dark depression that looked like an abcess and close to the lip lay the body from which my father had severed the head. We were almost overpowered by the reek as it was already putrifying.

'Stinking already and if the crows don't come soon, there'll be nothing except a few mouldy bones for them to fight over,' Bandicoot thought at my father. 'That's your entrance all right. A bloody bottomless pit right into the bowels of the earth and so large that even humans can pass through; but you have to take care, for this is almost an official entrance and is guarded, though how that creep managed to get by it I don't know.'

My father stared at the hole thoughtfully: 'So down the hole, he goes, does he? Well, I'll mark it out so that he'll know.'

It might have been a laughing matter – for him, but not for me. For him I was the invisible son; miffed, I watched him go through the charade of shifting the body so that its arms now indicated the hole in the earth. This he did for my benefit, despite me being there with him. And, not content with that, he piled up a small heap of earth on which he placed a flat stone with the thinner end pointing towards the blowhole. 'Well, that will guide him and I'll put similar signs along the way,' he said in the general direction of the old man.

'Good, now let's go and don't forget the head,' the old man replied, changing into the sleek form of Bandicoot and taking to the air. Jangamuttuk became Goanna and joined him. Before darting away, they swooped over the entrance to the underground and there was a howl and Bandicoot darted away. Goanna lingered. A large dingo leapt up towards him. He flew off and the dingo went back to his lair. My father now landed at the body and added another sign, the paw of a dingo, whatever good that might do. I knew it was there and dingo or no dingo I didn't fancy my chances with that giant brute.

CHAPTER SIX

I stared after them as they took to the sky, then examined the hole down which I was supposed to go, keeping well away from it. Well, it would have to wait – I was hungry, tired and without the nerve to tackle that hazard as yet. So, I loped away to the edge of the plateau and descended, picking my way through the rocks and scrambling down the steep places. All four legs worked as well as if I had been a dingo all my life, but I was dog-tired by the time the ground levelled off. I was in the little niche in the plateau wall, made by the stream along whose bed I had descended. I pushed my way into the middle of a patch of brush to curl up and sleep. First things first, and when I awoke I would get some food and then decide about the hole and its awful guardian.

When I slept I dreamt of Wadawaka, my friend who was like an elder brother to me. I saw him within a vast cavern and with him – this was more than enough to jerk me awake – was my mistress. I gave a long low moaning groan which broke off as I gaped a great yawn – a yawn which for some unknown reason returned me to my human shape. I pushed my way out of the brush and stood up as George. I was dizzy with hunger and my guts rumbled for food. I looked up at the sun; it was past noon. Already afternoon and I had accomplished nothing, except backtracking myself. Still, that rumble in the guts needed to be satisfied. I must eat before resuming my quest. But getting tucker was easier thought than done.

First of all, I had to make a spear and hunt. I had seen and smelled lots of wallaby and kangaroo, but if I wanted to gorge on fresh red meat, I would have to make a spear.

I stared at the trees and the short trunks of the brushwood I had emerged from. There were shafts enough; but did I have the skill? First of all, I would have to select my sapling, hack it down, rip off the leaves and then hold the stick out from my eyes horizontally to check if it was straight enough. If my would-be shaft was crooked, I would have to heat it over a fire to slowly straighten it by bending it backwards and forwards until the shaft would fly true; but to do this I had to build a fire and to do that I would have to find the correct stones to strike together or use the wooden drill method. Of course, while I was hunting for the stones, I could also find one to scrape the bark and boughs from the sapling and another to be chipped into a spear point. It was then that I decided that this living in the wilderness as a human wasn't going to be easy and that really to survive I had to become Dingo, he who was armed with the necessary weapons and cunning to pull down any animal.

And so I willed myself into him. My senses sharpened as the colour of the world leached away into sharp movements of black on a vacant white screen. Now the whole bush was filled with an overpowering cacophony of sounds and voices. I ignored them to sniff up the smells and separated them out until I found the gentle scent of wallaby and the harsher one of kangaroo. And then I found another scent, that of my father. What was he doing there? Even though I was almost dying of hunger, I put my nose to the ground and went after him, almost retracing my former route from the plateau. Then there came to me the smell of food, the putrid but mouth-watering stink of rotting flesh.

There in front of me, gazing at me with shifting eyes was the human head my father had stuck on a short stake. I trotted forward and as I reached it, a swarm of flies arose from where the eyes had been. It was their green shining bodies that I had mistaken as the glittering gaze of the eyes.

I sniffed at the face. My stomach growled in a putrid breath and I snapped the nose away and began to gnaw on it, coming to the ground to do so, and as I did I saw human sign and silly sign at that. It was only that of my father reminding me of the quest and so I gulped down the nose, then snapped at the head. It tumbled onto the ground and I went to work stripping off the cheek flesh while I thought of what my father had left me: a short stick pointing away, and at what? At the plateau and that bloody hole up there into which I had to go, that is if I made it past that brute of a devil dingo who most likely had it in for any other male dingo. I groaned as I broke into a lope towards the niche in the wall of the escarpment which I knew led up to the plateau and if it was flat enough and had water enough there I would be able to get at a 'roo or a wallaby. I needed sustenance if I was to continue the quest, for the scraps I had had off that rotting human head had only tickled my taste buds.

As I loped into the canyon there came to me the musky smell of a bandicoot and I snuffed it up, together with the strong human smell of my father. I really hadn't got far today and was back at the camp of that old codger. I continued past his camp and on to scramble back up the rocky dry stream bed. It was hard going up and my paws started hurting, but I went on, for my stomach was paining me far worse.

By the time the land flattened, I was limping. I stopped, sat and raised my snout to sniff the air. Somewhere along the stream bed was water, so I continued on. The plain was dry and the water course littered with pebbles and rocks. It wasn't much of a place and as for water, well, there was only that single smell coming to me. I limped on through the rocks and pebbles (many of which I swear shone with the signs of that yellow metal) towards where the sun was descending to its camp in the west. Soon it would fall beneath the earth, but that didn't worry me, for as a dingo the night was as the day and would be better for the hunting I was about to do. The water source was very near; I saw there a small pool, redolent with the scent of food. I immediately dropped to my belly and settled down, hoping that the moans from my empty stomach would not give me away, or that the tiredness would not hinder me when the time came to make my kill. I had not long to wait. There lingered at the edge of the pool a number of kangaroo families. The kids would make a nice meal. My saliva bubbled at the thought of the greens within their stomachs. Pot liquor! But I did not rush in, I took it easy as my father had told me to do when on the hunt.

At last, I was ready to make my move. I tensed and sprang, right at the throat of a joey. I ripped at its windpipe, then turned and raced at the adult kangaroos who, alarmed, leaped away in a confused mob. I kept after them for a few seconds before my tiredness swept over me, then swung about to get my prey. What matter if she was shuddering in her death throes? Her blood would be all the better for that. The blood pulsated from the gaping wound I had ripped in her throat – such a waste. I thrust my muzzle into the wound stopping the precious fluid from escaping, letting it flow instead down my relaxed throat and feeling it release its energy into my own veins. At last, I sucked up the last drops, then stopped and turned, gazing about for any enemies as well as listening and sniffing before going to the water's edge, drinking and returning to my meal. With my incisors, I peeled back the fur and skin over the stomach area, then ripped into the flesh and feasted on the intestines and the contents. I picked at my meal until I was full and then wished to nap; but now my quest was urgent in my mind. Much of the joey remained and as the animal itself was too big for me as a dingo to carry or drag, I again became George and slung the animal on my shoulder and went towards where I thought the hole was.

Soon, my human nose detected a putrid smell of rotting flesh and I knew that this marked my goal. As I neared, there were squawking protests from a flock of crows which had been feasting on the headless corpse of Strongarm's younger brother. I dropped my load, then picked up stones, shying them at the birds and driving them away. Perhaps I was thinking about burying him; but I grew accustomed to the smell and bent over the body and lo and behold, what did I see, but those signs that my father had made. Well, it must've been part of the ritual, I thought as I saw one pointing towards the low bank of earth beyond which lay my destination. Thinking only of stashing my kangaroo carcass a little beyond the corpse so that the crows would not get at it too much, I ambled to the bank and went up to see what I could see. I didn't make it to the top, for the giant devil dingo flashed into my mind just as he flashed into my sight and hearing. Its great bellow of a voice sent me reeling back down the bank and past the body. It was some time before I summoned up enough nerve to go back even as far as the corpse.

There I stared at the huge paw mark which my father had drawn. Ah, yes, the damned quest – and how was I to get past that bloody animal and down the hole? Even if I became Dingo, I would not be strong enough to challenge such a monster whose slavering jaws as he poked his head out of the hole seemed wide enough to swallow me whole, either as human or dog.

At a loss as to what to do, I wandered around the circular embankment and saw where the watercourse ran to or away from the hole. It had cut a deep gully into the bank and if I could lure the animal down there for a time, I might dash to the hole and descend before he realised it – although he might still follow my scent. I had to disguise it. I went back to the body with its overpowering reek. Angrily, I chased the crows away from it and from my joey which I carried to the lip of the bank, keeping down so that the giant devil dingo could not see me. It did, however, smell me or the dead joey for there came a snarl that shook the ground. At least the brute was hungry.

I went back to the corpse and lifted it up. Juices dripped from it and over me, effectively disguising my smell. I made my way along the gully carved in the bank by the water and was glad to find that it was deep enough to hide me. Now I crept up the bank and towards the hole. The giant devil dingo poked its head out and I stood still. It gave a great bellow and charged out. I shivered at the sight of those slavering jaws and fell backwards into the gully and thus out of his view. He did not follow, but I had to lure him out if I was to go down that bloody hole. The crows had ripped and pecked at the corpse and patches of flesh and skin hung loose. I yanked two largish pieces off and climbed to the top of the bank, flung one at the hole. The brute's head flashed out and the morsel disappeared down his gullet. It whetted his appetite. He came out with a rush. I flung the next piece down into the gully and he went past me in a flash. I heard him rending the corpse apart. Quickly, I picked up my kangaroo and dashed to the hole. I flung the carcass into it and then myself. The sides were steep, but I found a handhold, then another, there were enough cracks and ledges for me to make my way down swiftly. I almost fell down in my haste, but was far down by the time the giant devil dingo's head appeared to block out the entrance light. I saw that he was too big and clumsy to climb down and get at me, so I stopped on a ledge to shout my defiance at him. He bellowed back, but that was merely noise. His voice echoed about me as I continued my descent. So much for the giant devil dingo, but what else might I come across down here?

CHAPTER SEVEN

I felt the rough stony surface under my gripping toes, my fingers reaching out for tiny crevices to cling to as I descended down that rocky gullet. The O of the open mouth was just a tiny roundness of light above me and if it had not been for the phosphorescent glow from the stone walls I would have been in complete darkness. But then there was not much to see. Better to be a feeling creature, seeking out the hand- and footholds by a sense that was becoming more and more acute as the skin wore from my fingers and toes. How my body ached! I was already tired of this incessant descent; but it dominated me and I kept at it with an obsessive intensity. Fingers clinging, toes seeking out slight indentations to take my weight, feeling down for the next ledge or crack, frightened of falling, feeling a warm wind emerging from the hole. Too tired to go on; but I had to go on, ever downwards, from handhold to handhold, toehold to toehold. Toes blistering, then raw; fingers the same way, wanting to rest, but there was nowhere for me to linger. I paused at last, hanging there in a weakness that threatened to plunge me to my doom, then strength came to me from without, for my younger brother, Augustus, he who fell from the mast while we were still in sight of our island, appeared to guide me. It was he who placed my toes securely, pointed out slight protuberances on the rock to which I could cling, and it was he who led me diagonally down and across the curve of the gullet to where there was a ledge wide enough for me to lay down and rest, then sleep. I dreamed while he watched over me.

Again I was with my friend, Wadawaka, and my mistress deep within the earth, in a vast cavern lit with glowing pools of liquid which reflected off myriad specks of mitre in the walls and ceiling to make it a magical place, warm and secure; but all was not well in that refuge. Something was wrong with him. His face was both blank and strained and stress lines mottled his eye sockets and wrinkled his brow. As for my mistress, she seemed more at ease. Her face was calm, free of lines, but like that of a doll fixed in one expression. It was her voice which was fluid, unrolling in a breathless monotone in my mind.

Her toneless voice droned on, drawing me into her in sympathy. 'Here I am queen of this underground,' she declared without passion. 'Here I am far from the sun and in full command, thus I am a queen and what does a queen need but a king.' Her voice grew passionate as she spoke of and to Wadawaka. 'Once, I saw you as a footman, or a body servant. I was a lady and you were at my beck and call, but I am beyond that now. This country and this place has leached such thoughts of caste from my mind. Even then, when I was in the old country and held such ideas, what was I but a callow girl waiting to be turned. He came, my first dark lord and when he had finished with me, I was no longer what I had been.' Her voice rose in an anguish: 'But why did he have to abandon me, his newly made creature, alone and constantly in danger from my need to slake my thirst? Was it a time of testing? I was tested, believe me.' Now her voice dropped: 'Still, I have survived and descended to this place where I am free from the sun and those who might do me harm. Here I am and so are you, my love, for I have chosen you as my new dark lord, and all that I ask is that you accept me as I love you – you, a thing of darkness as I am.

But what is wrong with you? You do not speak and your face is twisted as if you hate me. How can we be enemies, when we are similar? I know you, for your mind is open to me; so my love, accept your lot and I shan't change you, though there is no earth in you and how could I change such a liquid thing? You were born on the sea and your blood is not to my taste, though I would never have supped on you unless you freely offered me your neck. Speak, I command you!' she suddenly shrieked, her voice setting up great echoes in the vast cavern.

Her voice dropped again. 'Yes, my dear, you have to learn that there are other things than the freedom of the ocean; then this underground will be your paradise. You want to flee, do you?! You know what happens to runaway slaves? No, forgive me and I shall be patient, and wait until you assume your kingship willingly and rule with me. Look around you. See how wide and vast our kingdom is. There are tunnels stretching far and wide and in them I have sensed strange beasts which we can hunt when you truly become my lord. And if these underground spaces are not to your liking, then there are those above ground, and there we can pursue our prey. Their blood is perfumed and deeply satisfying; but first bind your mind with mine and make this your home. Love me and I shall give you children to grace your knee. Hear their sweet prattling voices; how they do go on, they need a doggy to distract them and he is coming right now. I am calling him to us. Soon we shall be a real family and rule this place as a family. Now, my dark lord caress me, for you and I should be one in all things ...'

Her voice stopped, but her mind became my mind. I stared through her eyes at the black naked body of my friend and then looked down at her/my own body, pale and lithe and tense with the urges that drove me on, wailing through the dark night of her soul. We were sitting in a warm pool of water; but never could I be warm, not even when I caressed him and we joined, I was a thing of darkness and cold.

Desperately, I sought to find a warmth in him. If only he would speak, if only the tropic warmth of his sea would flow over and into me; but all I could sense was the wintry whip of the ocean-hurled spray and the sudden icy howl of the gale that drove me into a frenzy, until I hurled over the climax and sunk onto his chest, listening to the sound of the waves moving through his body. I pressed my ear to his chest and my hunger grew as I heard the thudding of his heart driving his rich blood through his arteries. I wished to extend my eye teeth and gently pierce through into that ruby stream and let it flow into my mouth; but I knew that his blood was not to my liking and if I would feed, I must do it from someone else – and how could I have these urges to drain him dry when he was my dark lord? I did not want him as sustenance nor did I want to claim him as a slave. No, there were slaves enough to sustain me in the world above. I needed him as my lord and if only he could become reconciled to this new land, he could rule it at my side.

Well, he would come around, for I know what binds male and female together: children! It is as a father that a man enters into responsibilities and ends his roaming. I will give him a man child and a woman child and thus a family. How warm I suddenly feel. Perhaps it is the water, though I cannot sense if it be hot or cold. The warmth comes from within me and flows out to him who will share my life down here. How hot his body is, a fit container for my feelings. How firm the slab of his chest; the strength of his thighs and loins; the surge of his blood, and I am famished and need to feed ...

I was pulled from this scene and from my sleep by a tugging at my side. I rubbed my eyes and stared about, hating the place in which I found myself. I shuddered perilously on a thin ledge which overhung a bottomless pit. Worse, my mistress's hunger had aroused in me a similar hunger. I needed to eat. This drove me off the ledge and down. I was relieved to find that the crevasse began to level out into a rocky floor and then I was overjoyed to find the carcass of the joey I had flung into the pit the other day, or month, or what have you, for without the sun and moon and stars, time had no meaning here.

I stared down at the remains of the kangaroo, my saliva rising. I was so hungry I drooled as I tore at the meat with my fingers. Being completely naked I had no knife; but who needed anything when I could change to Dingo and rip off strips of flesh with my fangs. I snarled and growled as I worried the carcass and gulped down the rancid meat. By the time I was through, there was only enough for another meal, though I had left some of the organs in the chest cavity. These would make a choice snack later, but to carry the remains I changed back to George and slung the skeletal remains across my shoulder.

As the tunnel continued at an incline I could walk without scrabbling with my poor scabby fingers and toes. I simply strolled on with the stripped joey on my shoulder and much of his flesh in my belly. I don't know for how long I had been walking when there came the sound of rushing water which made me realise I was thirsty and had been for some long time. In fact, the congealed blood in the carcass had added to my thirst, not alleviated it. I hurried forward ready to have a long and satisfying drink. But the stream was further away than I had judged and I was on the verge of becoming Dingo to make more haste, when the walls of the tunnel turned left and right and in front of me were the banks of a fast flowing dark river. I dropped the carcass and knelt down, lowering my face until my mouth made contact with the water. I gulped up the slightly warm and sulphur-tasting fluid with rising bubbles that tickled my nose and eventually made me draw back with a resounding sneeze.

I was now satisfied by both food and drink and sat back to contemplate the dark stream which seemed to bar my way forward. I looked across the stream at the rocky wall and thought that with my luck, this would eventually happen to the rocky shelf on my side. It was then I heard the plash of paddles.

I listened carefully, cupping a hand about one ear while closing off the other with my fingers, so that I might find the direction from which it was coming. Someone was paddling across the current towards me. I stayed where I was, watching until a low dugout canoe glided to the bank. I knew the paddler. It was the blackfellow of many names and few abilities, though each name signified a skill. When we had met, he had called himself Spirit Master, and as I looked at him I saw that he was even more hideous than he had been then. His face was as grey as that of a corpse and his mouth kept opening and closing in a continuous gulping. He sat twisted in an ungainly heap for a long minute, his bulging eyes almost starting from their sockets as he swivelled them about without moving his head. They fell on me and held. He began speaking in a wet voice which splattered drops of spit onto his lap, for he did not raise his face to me.

'Well here I am,' he spluttered. 'And here are you, a boy, though I was expecting something more to my taste. Well, it can't be helped. One meal is as good as another, as long as the meat is rotting off the bones. And what is that I smell, what is that from upstairs? Hard to get it down here. Doesn't matter, yes, it does. Everything matters. I matter, you matter, my job matters. I am the famous Spirit Master now renamed, the Ferryman of

Souls, the one and only, Renfie, once also known as the Singer of Whales. Those who wish to enter my underground must enlist my aid, a difficult thing indeed, for I do nothing for nothing and those who usually come here have no fare and thus fare badly. So hand it over. Pay or go or stay, or dive into the water and swim or float, meet those things in the water which will hasten your journey straight down their gullets. But enough of this. Only the dead may enter here, so first, are you dead?'

'Am I dead,' I replied. 'In this grave hole and you ask that. What else could I be?'

'Alive and food; but let me test you, though your smell is rank enough,' drooled the ferryman, struggling out of the canoe and falling towards me with a horrible sideways lurching that put me in a mind to flee. 'Now, let me see,' he spluttered, globs of spit hitting my naked body as he leant forward and sniffed at me. His blob of a misshapen nose moved along my body slowly and held on my crotch. He took in a great long drawn breath, held it for a long moment, then expelled it and declared: 'You have the stink of death about you and your soul is as shrivelled as that thing between your legs.'

'I do indeed,' I replied, remembering how I lifted the headless body to throw as a distraction to the giant devil dingo and how it had been swollen with a decay that oozed all over me.

'Yes, I am dead to the overground,' I told him with a quaver in my voice, not from death itself, but from the stink of putrefaction which writhed from him in visible vapour trails. He was so rank that I wondered how he could smell anything beyond that of his own stench.

'There is still the fare which must be paid,' he said with a leer and a grimace which almost made me retreat once and forever from this monster even though I was on a quest to rescue my friend. I had to control my dismay, dislike and fear as he spluttered on. 'I am not here because I am on a river cruise,' he said, 'but because I am the official ferryman, one whom you once knew as Spirit Master, once Singer of Whales, with the secret name of Renfie. Give me the fare and we'll be on our way; but don't expect a commentary on the sights and scenes as we go along, for there isn't much to be seen.'

What could I give him, I thought in despair. After all I was completely naked and could carry nothing. Then I remembered the carcass of the kangaroo and dumped it in front of him.

'There,' I told the misshapen thing, 'there is your fee, so take it and let me aboard.'

'What is that, what is that? Why that is, that is kangaroo, and young and green. I like them just like that, the juices smearing my chops as I gulp down the flesh tender with rot. Let me hope that there are maggots too. Now let me see, if it will do.'

He thrust a hand into the ripped stomach and shoved it up into the chest cavity. 'Arrh,' he exclaimed and came out with an oozing fist closed about the heart of the joey. He stuffed it into his mouth and noisily chewed it. Pieces splattered out as he commented: 'Tasty and tender. It melts in the mouth. Now let me see what else is in there.' He poked his hand again into the carcass and took his time in feeling about. 'The intestines are gone, but, ah, liver, kidney, lungs and is that the uterus. Better, though not as good as testicles, still! Enough, get on, get on and we'll be off.'

Holding the carcass close to his chest, he did that half falling sideways lurch that ended with him slumped over in the canoe. The craft rocked dangerously as if it might overturn, but he growled and it became still. 'Right, get in. Not at the stern, idiot. At the bow so that I can keep an eye on you. This meat is mine and I don't want you gnawing on it behind my back.'

I gingerly clambered in and sat in trepidation at the bow as he had directed. He growled again and the canoe shot into midstream. The current took us and rushed us away. 'Lucky, lucky, no paddling here,' he cackled, adding another hideous sound to his collection. 'This river goes around and around. Drop a body overboard and it'll come back to you in time. Now let me have a snack on that virgin uterus ...'

I had to listen to the creature slobbering over the bits and pieces that I had kept to snack on later, as the canoe rushed along the dark stream which indeed filled the tunnel from side to side and even began rising towards the ceiling. Then he started gnawing on the ribs and every now and again there was a splash as he flung a bone overboard. At last, he finished his repast and there was silence except for the rushing of the water. I must have dozed off, for the next thing I became conscious of was the canoe rocking as the ferryman shifted towards me. His hand reached out. His touch was cold and clammy. I recoiled and instantly changed into Dingo and leapt into the air. But my power of flight had left me and I fell into the water and the current immediately swept me away from the canoe.

'There is worse than me out there, far worse,' he snarled. 'I am Ferryman of Souls, but there are eaters of souls in that water and they will get you. Well, I just wish that I could watch.' It was then that he stopped and began wailing: 'Come back, get back here. She wants you with her. Please, she is a shrew and hates to be crossed. Come, come, take the paddle and I'll pull you aboard.' But by then I was too far from the canoe and his curses receded away from me. At the mercy of the dark current I was carried deeper into the earth. So much for the Ferryman of Souls I thought as I found myself alone in the swirling blackness.

CHAPTER EIGHT

It was a relief to get away from him and enjoyable bathing in the water which was warm flowing over my body. Not a thing nibbled at my toes or tried to swallow me. I let myself be pushed along by the tepid sulphurish smelling liquid that held me up like the waters of the Dead Sea and even changed back to George so that he could have a good bath and clear himself of the putrid muck from the corpse. It was hard to submerge completely and I bobbed on like a cork as both tunnel and stream grew more sultry. At last, the current had had enough of me and drove me against a ledge of rock onto which I rolled. I dozed off immediately and fell from consciousness into a dream-like state, one which was mercifully blank until the shook-shook sound of giant bat wings hovered directly over me with glaring red eyes. A hand stroked me into pleasure as a gentle voice spoke kindly. I was drawn out of that trance-state and into the mind of my mistress. I gave a whimper of delight and, dog or human, I wished to lick her hand in gratitude and love. I was well and truly tamed – her pet!

Now, on leathern wings, we flew through the cavern, then swirled up and up to where a chimney led to the surface. How we exulted in the star-studded sky and the vast reaches of the night before I felt myself absorbed or merged in her. I hurtled downwards from the friendly reaches of the sky to where, in a niche between rocky walls, a fire was burning fitfully. I swooped low and saw two small figures stretched out on the ground beneath a blanket of stitched together possum skins.

I landed and assumed my human form, standing there a moment as I re-inhabited my human shape. I ran my hands over my firm thighs and ruffled the vee of pubic hair so light and whispery. I felt the curve of my breasts and tossed my head so that my blonde hair swung out and back around my gaunt face. This was where that old blind savage spent his days, but this night not even a smell of him. What matter, I have no need to play with him. Such an old fool! Still, he did give me some amusement. It was fun to run my hands over his face and then skip back as he came awake with a rush to querulously challenge my presence. Even better was to press myself against him and rub my breasts over his withered old hairy chest. That really got him going and the last time I had done that, the old dotard had flung a spear at me, missing of course, and in return I had planted a resounding kiss on his parched lips, then with a mocking laugh I changed into Bat, fluttered my wings in his face, then ascended into the sky, rising higher and higher, before gliding away from the dawning day, down the vertical passageway to my home and man.

Curiously, I now examined the small shapes beneath the rugs and to my joy, found two native children. Gently, I lifted the blanket and examined their naked forms – two boy infants of about five years old huddled together as the rug was taken from them. I dropped it back and felt myself smiling as I had not done for many days. Indeed, I felt as a mother to these little ones and they were what I needed to bind my man to me.

I kissed their sleeping faces, assumed my bat shape and skimmed off into the air. I needed to feed before the night was done.

As I was rising up I saw something that disturbed me, for it meant that if I was caught they would make an end of me. I landed, becoming my girlish shape and stared at the object. Not so long ago, in the course of my passion, I had accidentally turned one of the natives and thus made a competitor for my food supply. He had run off and I had let him go as a thing of no consequence. Now, someone had found him enough of a threat to murder him. There was his head rotting beside the stake upon which it had sat. It had been there for a night or two and the crows had been at work. Where his eyes had been were two gaping holes and his cheeks had been ripped away. I shuddered as I stared at the remains of what had been a thing like me. Now it was nothing but a rotting head. What would I be if I were caught. I was old, ancient, and would fall into a pile of rancid dust if the point of a wooden spear pierced me through and through into the heart. And would they take my skull, the bare bones without flesh and stick it upon a stake to warn others of my kind? They would, they would, and since they have little mercy for me, I will have none for them!

Poor thing, I might have buried the head, if the ground had not been hard and if I had not been interrupted by the distant sound of a native ceremony which seemed – no, which was – familiar! I recognised the chanting voice and a desire for revenge came rushing up. I didn't want his blood; I wanted his life! That old savage had thwarted me before, but he would not again! I listened to the crack-crack of his clapsticks and it signified the snap of his neck and each and every single bone in his body. The thud-thud of bare feet upon the ground was but I tossing his broken body hither and thither. As I listened, I found a use for that head. I pulled out the stake. Blood had dried upon it and the fluids of decay had dripped down upon it. I jammed it into the neck and held it up. The wood became slick with juice and maggots tumbled onto my hand. I held death in my hand and laughed, for if I had been disturbed by its sight how would the savages take the sight of one of their number filled with maggots and stinking, stinking to high heaven!

'*Wolla koorpana kooloo waroo*,' strong males, thick with rich red blood, sang in time to the clapsticks.

His voice, a rattle of phlegm in an aged throat, bloodlessly chanted in reply: '*Meun korunna linja rooeri. Mean korunna weat yorinni.*'

Standing at the edge of the clearing, I could see the old coot performing his perfidious rites and rituals. He danced like a scarecrow and was decorated like, what else but a savage. He had two long red bands gleaming like wet blood across his forehead. They dripped down the sides of his neck and body to his thighs. His grey patch of pubic hair and old circumcised prick were partially covered by a large flat seashell and about his skinny shanks were wrapped bark and leaves. He had on amulets of some sort of skin decorated with white feathers and he waved about a forked wand on the ends of which had been fastened sharp pieces of bone. Bone could not harm me!

I watched him stamp out a vicious dance with a rhythm like the two-step of marching soldiers. He stamped first his right foot, then his left, ducked down in a half squat, then sprang up and vibrated his skinny highs. He was a farce; but not so the other male dancers who were all tossing turgid penises. So much for their dirty games, I thought, as without further ado I flung the head into the centre of them, then flashed into my bat shape and darted off and up to the top of one of the two rock columns which was in darkness. The ceremony was being held between them and the fires which had been lit at the points of the compass did not shed enough light to illuminate where I now perched – on a ledge half way up the column, a safe vantage point from which to observe the effect of the head which had struck the old codger, then landed at his feet. It was also the perfect spot from which to launch an attack.

I choked off a wild shriek of delight for after a startled minute of silence there followed panic. 'It is my younger brother,' screamed a big man from where he had been sitting. He jumped to his feet and collapsed before the head, wailing out a wordless dirge. This set the females off. I examined them for a blood-filled victim while they wailed on. Then came male shouts, followed by muttering and shifting of positions as the savages divided into two hostile groups, the smaller one I was happy to see was led by my old enemy. The large group clustered leaderless, until the big fellow whom I had my eye on for my meal, stopped his whining and got to his feet to give a virile cry. I would enjoy him especially as the shout was directed at the vile old man. I would whisper my thanks in his ear as I took his blood.

'That Milyado bogus shaman first brought evil upon us,' he screamed. 'Now this old villain has done the same.' He rushed off and charged back with a long, long spear. The men of his group followed his example. I waited for them to begin fighting. In the melee I would make my choice and suck him; but then, I saw that the old coot's group was unarmed, except for one, a giant brute of a man who if I could get at him would fill my mouth and body with all of his powerful strength. He had been and was so sure of himself that though he had been sitting next to the man (my other choice for a meal) who had declared the head to be that of his brother, he had not moved during the commotion. Now, he got to his feet and I saw that he carried a worthy weapon. The sight of it threatened to make me forget all caution. I needed to feast and I would. I jerked off the ledge and fell down, spreading my wings at the last moment to glide down beside the dance ground and near a path which led from there to the camp. I knew it well enough, for I had taken that younger brother there and had found him good, though not excellent. Now such was my need that the first to come would be mine.

I had not long to wait. There was a pounding of feet and a native came rushing along the path. As he reached my position, I stepped onto the track and stopped him with the power of my eyes. I pulled him off the path at the same time knocking his wooden tipped spear from his grasp. He stood there trembling as I stroked him, just as I do my dog, before kneeling in front of him and taking him into my mouth. I wanted to linger over my repast, take one then the other; but my thirst together with the shouting and screaming from the dance ground made me hasten. He gave a short despairing shriek as my fangs sank into him. I lapped up his rich red fluid so tangy with the taste of eucalyptus. This was followed by a scream as I forgot all caution and tore at him and drained him of both the red and white. How sweet and tart he tasted as he died in my arms. I held him tightly until he was still then, getting up, I carried him to the edge of the dance ground. There stood that giant of a man with his giant of a weapon. How I wished it was from him that I had drunk. I flung the drained and mutilated carcass at him. He batted it away as if it was a ball and this set the other group to howling.

Now would come the fun as they tore at each other's throats, I anticipated as I hid in the shadows, licking away at the fluids smearing my lips, savoring both the metallic and doughy tastes blended together. With a scream as shrill as that from any victim I had toyed with, the brother of the head raised his spear and hurled it at the giant. He brushed it aside easily as he ran forward to fell him with a single blow of his club. Now it was on, but with the leader down and the big man so completely in control, the group led by the old coot were able to make their way to the sea with him as a rearguard. The unconscious one lay where he had fallen and I was about to descend on him to send him to his brother, when there was a wailing and a group of women rushed to surround his unconscious form. Thus foiled, I trailed after the warring parties to the beach, hoping to see some bloody action.

At the beach I saw an island to which the old man's party might retreat, but they were trapped as the locals spread out to engulf them on three sides. Not wanting to be discovered and having had my meal, I assumed my bat form and heavy with blood lumbered into the air searching for a vantage point from which to watch the massacre. Alas it was not to be. In the air I saw that the island was connected to the mainland by a rocky causeway and, as I watched, the old man and his group rushed across. Too late, the local group charged up the beach. They halted at the foot of the causeway screaming defiance and flinging their spears harmlessly across the water. The old man's lot jeered them from the island, and that was that. There was no attempt at pursuit and, disappointed, I rose up in the air and flew away as the night was edging towards the dawn.

Well, the old man would keep and this was proper for it was said that vengeance was a dish best taken cold. I reached the camp and even that old fellow was not there. Without him to hinder me, I retrieved my precious burden even though day was approaching and the nearest entrance was some way away. As a new mother, not even the threat of annihilation would keep me away from my little ones, and I hugged them to me fiercely as I bent my head to take a snack. I was feeling somewhat weak from the events of the night.

CHAPTER NINE

I was a kid then, not used to the drinking of blood and other things. My mistress's experiences sickened me, even though I could tell myself that I was merely a spectator and never would personally engage in such things. Well, kids are kids because their minds are simple and open to sweet corruptions. I was attached to my mistress and loved her even though I didn't like the idea of her going after my father; but, then, he was more than a match for her and safely back on the island. After all, I was the one on the quest and in danger. But for all my evasive thinking, I still felt defiled and scrubbed my body in the tepid stream as if I might purify myself, though the warmth and smell was very much like blood. It did not help my peace of mind either that I was famished and the memory feeling of my mistress filling herself up so that the fluids dribbled from her mouth did not repel me so much as make me long to do the same with rich red meat. I scrubbed on, trying to keep my mind on my task; but I was remembering my mistress's reddened eyes, her hand on me and her rapacious feeding. I needed food!

The growling and rumbling of my belly changed me into Dingo. I trotted off along the tunnel leading off the ledge, hoping that along it I might encounter something I could get my teeth into. I padded eagerly, but scented nothing but her, my mistress. This caused me to increase my speed for I knew that food should be where she was. I ran along the trail with my nose not to the ground, but high in the air, for that was where her odour lingered.

Suddenly, I stopped my headlong pace. The illumination from the walls had petered out and ahead was pitch blackness. As a human, I might have forced myself on, but to a young dingo, the utter darkness was frightening. How could I blunder through it, not knowing what danger lurked there? But I was human as well as animal and I pushed down any feral fright, knowing that being Dingo with my heightened senses, I could continue along, guided by her scent. Who needed eyes when I had such sharp senses of smell and hearing? I trotted forward into the darkness warily, my ears pricked and shifting from side to side, my nose twitching for any smells beyond that of the familiar.

The darkness was a felt thickness and even in my Dreaming animal shape, I walked on verging on a panic. I sensed the ghosts of my mob shuffling along beside me. My nose smelled only death and decay. As if from afar, my ears caught the droning of Wawilak's didjeridoo. It yelped out the sound of a dog in distress. My hackles rose; but all I could do was creep towards the distress signal, ready to turn and run. Then the pitch darkness seemed to give and I saw Wawilak sitting there, his long rod of wood to his bearded lips; but how could it be when one night, a night almost as dark as the tunnel, he had vanished from our vessel, presumably fallen overboard and drowned, though even when we beat back on our wake, there was no trace of his body. There also came to me the familiar scent of Augustus my brother and I even felt the touch of his hand for a brief instant, before the felt presence of these phantoms disappeared along with the feeling of containment. I was alone in what seemed like a vast emptiness. I barked once, twice, a third time, and the sounds sped away from my ears and returned faintly seconds later. I knew then that I was in a huge cavern and filled by the smell of ancient bones. They were even under my feet and such was my hunger that I lowered my head to gnaw at one huge bone which fell to dust in my mouth.

They were ancient and too dry for any nourishment, but I tried another and this turned out to be as hard as stone. Disappointedly, I stared and sniffed and listened, turning my head, eyes and ears all about until I saw a glimmer of light in the distance. I moved across the cavern towards it and entered a narrow side passage with walls glittering from embedded specks of mitre. As I walked down the passage too, the stone began to glow with some sort of whitish light which enabled me to break into a trot; but was this any better than the all encompassing darkness? Even the scent of my mistress had disappeared and I felt that I was the only living thing that ever had padded down this natural passageway. There were no phantoms here, no wailing sounds of the didjeridoo. I was crushed with my isolation and what might I have done to myself, if not at the very moment when my depression was at its deepest, I whimpered unconsciously and my own sound brought me to see ahead the whitish flicker of a figure coming towards me. What matter what it was as long as it shattered my solitude. I gave another whimper as I recognised the human shape, naked and with a pale white skin that glowed with an illumination of its own. Another phantom came to walk with me and my hackles rose and I gave a deep growl, bringing it all the way up from my chest, then she spoke and my tail wagged furiously in reply.

'Ah, my puppy dog has found me,' her sweet voice murmured and her gentle hand reached down to stroke behind my ears.

I jumped up in an ecstasy of welcome and she had to cuff me down. Even her blows added to my joy. My distress was over and I trotted happily at her side as she retraced her steps and we emerged into a vast cavern, this one thankfully illuminated. It stretched away to beyond the limits of my senses.

My mistress too must have felt lonely underground, for she was loquacious and spoke on and on in a low monotone as she walked along. 'It is as if once all this has been a sea,' she said either to me or to herself, but that did not matter, for her hand was on my head and how I loved her touch. 'See, my pet,' she murmured, addressing me directly, 'how along this cavern wall there are cliffs and promontories broken and weathered as if by ancient waves, and out on the flat floor of the cavern – why it must have been the bed of an ancient sea for there are cemented into the stone shells and the bones of strange sea creatures. This cavern is vast and I have not explored much of it, only wandered about the shores of this side. All along the stone wall are tunnels and chasms, in which things may lurk waiting for us to find them and now that I have a husband and a dog, we can begin to roam over our world and see what it holds for us. And if we find it empty, why we shall people it. Ah, to have subjects to do my bidding and perhaps, for my husband's sake, in our explorations, we shall come out onto the edge of a vast underground sea for which he can fashion a craft on which we can set sail. This is a new but ancient world,' she declared, her voice rising in exultation, 'it is mine by right of discovery and no-one can dispute my ownership.'

And so she went on, coating me with the murmuring of her voice until even I grew a little weary and worse, somewhat sorry for her; for the thought came to me that this immensity of space was but a vast trap girded over on all sides and what she and I really wanted was the sky with sun, moon and stars above us.

The entire cavern was illumined with a uniform light that lacked the dazzling brilliance of the sun, the gentle glow of the moon, or the shifting play of cloud shadows from the world above. Here, underground, the atmosphere was a clear, dry whiteness, warm and humid. The origins of such illumination, which was both of greater intensity but also less than the sun, I was at a loss to understand. I was so puzzled that I sat on my haunches and tried to think the problem through. I raised my snout and bayed at the tremendous vault above my head. What might be termed the sky shifted and writhed like luminous fog and beyond it I could see the immense arc of stone, but it was not so distant that I could not feel its heaviness and inertness. I shuddered and howled as I realised that it could come crashing down on my head.

'Come dog, stop that howling and come on,' called my mistress, giving a soft laugh as she realised what was disturbing me. 'Don't be a Chicken Licken, the roof is as strong as my will. Have no fear, if I decide to bring it down upon us, I'll give you plenty of warning.'

Reassured, I nuzzled her hand, then trotted along beside her. To our left was a huge hill of boulders piled up in a stupendous heap as if by the giants my father firmly believed in. I wondered if they had been here and if they were here still. It was a scary thought that the land my mistress thought was empty and uninhabited might be the home of these fabulous creatures. And worse still, that a tunnel might connect this underground with their fabled land far to the south where it was said the sun never shone.

'Silly savage tales,' her voice spoke in my head and ears. 'If they indeed were here, do you think that I would not know about such reservoirs of blood. Why, I could herd them like cattle and milk them like cows.' And she gave a cold laugh which drove such thoughts out of my head. I had other things to occupy my mind, important things – food and drink! I bounded forward to a limpid pool of water and thrust my snout at it. I drew back with a yelp with my nose burnt by the steaming water.

'No, no, try that one there, the water is cool and refreshing. You must be famished too, for there is little for a doggy to eat down here except fish.'

I went to the pool she had indicated. The water was tepid, but cooled my nose as I drank. My mistress continued on and by the time I raised my snout, she had disappeared. I ran along following her scent to where she had descended onto the dry bed of the sea to circle a steep promontory. It was then that I thought of flying, but as before when I had attempted to escape from the Ferryman of Souls, the sky was denied me. The loss of this ability evoked in me a sudden melancholy. I didn't want to be a landbound thing forever.

'Don't sulk,' my mistress's voice informed me. 'This is my kingdom and I have the power to give and to take away. You can sniff about on the ground for a while and when my husband has become more settled, then both of you shall have powers enough. So be faithful to me doggy and you shall see how kind I am.'

Her words didn't stop me from sulking and my spirits only revived when we turned the point of the promontory and there at its base began a forest with high and lofty trees with tufted tops like umbrellas. I dashed forward eager to hunt among the trunks, for surely things must live there, but when I ran beneath them I found no welcoming scents, only a dank earthy smell that almost put all thought of food out of my mind.

'Mushroom trees, doggy. Not to your liking I see. Don't worry, for we are almost home and there shall be a feast of fish for you. My husband is a great fisherman and even eats them raw.'

She led me to where a river had once divulged into the sea and we passed through an oval opening and into a grotto with magnificent stalagmites separating the space into rooms. The main floor had soft, silvery sand and there were ledges which might serve for sleeping spaces. Two of these were covered with soft moss and she pointed at a lower shelf and said: 'I'll make up that one for you. The rock is warm, but hard. Ah, and how are my little ones' she exclaimed affectedly, going to the smaller of the moss covered ledges.

What little ones I thought, padding over and putting my front paws on the ledge looking down. Two tiny black kids were lying there. I poked out a paw and they mewed and whimpered and stuck out their minute hands. The hands might have been small, but they weren't weak. Before I could jerk my head back, they had me by the ears and were dragging my head down towards their open mouths. 'The little darlings,' my mistress cluck-clucked, 'just like their mummy, aren't they?' And she undid their fingers from my ears and took them up. Immediately, they fastened on her breasts and began noisily sucking. I smelled the metallic scent of blood and felt I could do with a tit myself.

'How they drain one,' my mistress whispered tenderly, her face bending over the two tiny tykes. 'Don't you think they look like their father,' she added. 'How dark their skin and how greedily they suck. They will grow into strong men able to help us dominate this place. Now go and find the master. He will have fish for you. Go, scat, while I attend to my babies.'

My mistress played the mother, but there was something wrong and even distressing about the scene that caused me to whimper as I left the grotto to go to my friend. I snuffled about and found the sea smell of Wadawaka's scent and set off along it. Soon, I began to hear a soft crooning:

> Sometimes I feel that my race is almost done;
> Sometimes I feel that my race is almost done;
> I'm a long ways from my home.

And as I caught sight of him, his plaintive chant continued:

> Sometimes I feel like a motherless child;
> Sometimes I feel like a motherless child;
> A long ways from my home.

I reached him and tried to change back to George. Before it had been only a matter of wishing, but now as much as I tried I found that I could not. I remained Dingo and so it was as Dingo that I thrust my snout into his hand, then began licking it, hoping that he would speak to me and perhaps help me to effect the transformation. He stared down at me, but he had a blankness of eyes and face that alarmed me. It was as if his soul had been stolen from his body. He didn't even acknowledge my presence and all I could do was lie down at his side and wait for a sign of recognition. He turned away and stared at what he had been doing.

Here the rocky floor had dipped down and the hollow held a patch of earth. Along it in straight rows, Wadawaka had planted small mushrooms, each one spaced precisely apart. Now he examined his work then left me, uprooting one and shifting it a fraction. That done, he stood and began singing his dirge again. I felt the veil over his mind become opaque enough for me to peer through it, into a dim and dismal space. The wooden sides curved away and from above came hard shouts and thuds. I recognised the hold of a ship, but one arranged as I had not seen before. Along the sides were rows of wooden platforms on which were shackled black men and women. The air reeked with the smell of human waste and vomit. On one space lay a corpse and throughout the hold there was a continuous moaning and agroaning that made me growl in dismay and even anger. It was then that I saw her. A slim black woman with nappy hair clinging to her finely shaped skull and sloe-shaped eyes. She held a black baby, pressing it against her breast as she sang in a low monotone: 'Motherless children have a hard time, when mother is gone.' She held up the baby so that she could stare at it and her voice lifted into a lullaby.

> Hush little baby, don't you cry
> You know mother is about to die;
> All my trials will soon be over.

So overwhelming was the melancholy within his mind that I had to flee away and back into the cavern where things were starkly white and without shadows. My mate, Wadawaka, at least now was becoming aware of my presence. He stared down at me as if trying to recognise what I was, then without a word, he turned and walked off. I trotted after him, just like a dog. I too was changing here and barely aware of it.

He went to a pool and squatted at the edge. He had the patience of Job and remained still a long time, then at last his hand darted out and he flung a fish onto the bank. It was a fish I had not seen before, completely white all over and where its eyes should have been were two indentations. But my stomach had been tormenting me to distraction and I would not be put off by strangeness. It was tucker, a soggy boneless mess, but food for all that and I began gnawing at it as Wadawaka began his dirge again.

> *Sometimes I feel like a motherless child;*
> *Sometimes I feel like a motherless child;*
> *A long ways from my home.*

This seemed to relieve him and as I ate, I caught glimpses from his mind of the world above with its spill of ocean and towering waves and shrieking tempests. Wadawaka's hands clenched as if he held the helm of a vessel and was battling against the elements. I yelped in sympathy, then buried my nose into the innards of the fish. There was a rankness there that suddenly made me vomit up all the ill-smelling flesh I had eaten. I sniffed at my vomit, then at the remains and decided not to eat until I could find or be given something else. Better to starve I decided, than to eat such poisonous flesh. So began my time of fasting. I didn't eat a single thing, except that fish, all the time I was underground.

CHAPTER TEN

So there I was as a dingo famished and trapped underground, though it was, at least I thought so, where I wanted to be. After all I was at the end of my quest and I had come through as best as I could, although how I might extricate myself was another matter. I also had to rescue my friend, Wadawaka, who was needed to pilot our schooner to its destination. It would be difficult to get him away if he could not be aroused from his trance state. I would have to bring him to himself; but how? Jangamuttuk would know how, but he was not here. I wondered how he and my mob were faring while I was far from them, deep underground and in terrible danger. But then they had antagonised the local mob who now were after their blood, if I could use such a term. Still, my father was a shape changer and Hercules was more than a match for twenty or thirty men. I imagined what they might be up to and like all such dreams they were more in the nature of wish fulfilment, mere speculation than reality. Later, I learnt that at the time they were in conference and as in many such meetings Hercules dominated, whinging about this or that and threatening to wallop whoever or whatever was upsetting him.

'So let them come,' he growled, puffing his chest up, scowling and lifting his club, then thudding it down upon the ground. 'This time, the thick skull of Strongarm will shatter into a thousand pieces,' he bragged, bashing his waddy down again. It was crude, but we got the message.

My father, Jangamuttuk, had not become shaman and leader of our mob by being a Hercules and so he calmly regarded him, tugging at a burr which was entangled in his beard. He pulled it free and flicked it away, before replying: 'Strongarm and his mob are just as upset as we are. They are not the problem. Fighting them will do us no good at all. We have to get at the evil which is harming both groups and then we'll be able to go on. There is blood guilt to be allayed.'

'And what did I do, but exterminate a ghost who killed more than one of us and violated your wife's sisters,' Hercules shouted. 'I don't feel guilty, kill them all, I say. Let me at that Strongarm and down he'll go. I conquer or die.' Again his club thudded onto the ground in a gesture which was becoming tiresome.

'I feel that the female moma is the only threat to us,' Jangamuttuk replied. 'A devil who can't be stopped by a tap on the head. She's more than likely to rip away your club, then go for your throat.'

'Just let her try it. A female fighting against me. I've got another club for her,' he shouted as he fumbled at his pubic covering which did not quite cover his other large weapon.

'Yes, and that was the club my husband was talking about,' my mother, Ludjee, cut in. 'Look what she did to that blackfellow she flung into the boro ground. Watch out or she'll do the same to you. She must have a collection of those things and if she saw yours that night, she's after it. It is the biggest that I've ever seen and I bet the same goes for her,' she retorted, staring with measuring eyes at the giant's cock which most of the women had sampled. 'Best keep it hidden,' she added unable to stop a smile, though the situation was serious and she as a mother was suffering more than the others. She gave a sigh and her sisters began wailing in the background as she continued: 'I'm worried about my George. It was sending a boy on man's business. I don't know what got into my husband. Someone'll have to go after him. He can't rescue Wadawaka on his own.'

'Though sending Hercules would be sending a man on shaman's business,' Jangamuttuk commented dourly, somewhat put out by his wife's criticism. 'He's done his bit for us and can continue to do it – here! If he's here, there won't be any problems with that mob over yonder. They might think this island is taboo, but what happens if that Strongarm goads them across to attack us.'

'Yes,' declared Hercules. 'I am waiting to meet that Strongarm again. You blackfellows don't have to worry about him or them. They are mine. I'll take them all on.' And naturally, his club thudded down again.

'Well, that job is for you and the other needs to be done by a shaman anyway. The quest must be completed,' Jangamuttuk observed, 'and if I need help then there is my wife. She also has the necessary skills and both of us should be more than enough for a weak white thing like that.'

'Well, I've met that weak white thing,' put in Ludjee, 'and she will take some getting rid of.'

'Yeah,' Hercules replied, unimpressed: 'Well, off with you. I want to do a spot of hunting on this island shaped like a goanna, but covered with kangaroo droppings. Go, so we can be off; but get back quickly, or I'll come after you and give that thing a bashing.'

Having spoken, he thudded down his waddy and let it fall from his hands. He took up a heavy hunting spear, hefted it to check its balance, then without another word stalked off. The rest of the men after glancing at Jangamuttuk and receiving his nod went off after him.

My father and mother went on their own towards the causeway. It was high tide, but they had no intention of crossing the narrow stretch of water either by swimming or walking. They stood looking across at the mainland; there was a shimmer and where there had been my father now squatted a huge goanna with faded markings on his back. He flickered a tongue at the woman who stood beside him and she waded into the water until it reached the tops of her breasts and they floated in front of her. She began swimming, then suddenly threw up her arms and sank beneath the waves. Her disappearance was followed by an eruption of water and a large manta ray leapt up into the air. She exuberantly circled the island with a great flapping of wings then dove back into the ocean and came into the shallows where the giant goanna waited. He rose into the sky and she joined him and they turned to fly inland towards the serrated edge of the escarpment.

When they reached it, they turned and flew along the edge until they came to where there was an indentation in the wall. Goanna glided down and landed there. Manta Ray flopped down beside him and became human again. Goanna hesitated a second before transforming back into Jangamuttuk. Now they both walked towards where a few tendrils of smoke drifted up. Beside the few remaining coals of the fire sat old Milyado, or Bandicoot, and as always he was muttering away to himself and to whatever might be listening.

'Well, they would leave their kids with me, a blind old man who can hardly take care of himself. He wasn't invited to the ceremony, was he? Well, they got what they deserved. I'm the one who needs the looking after, not me looking after a couple of toddlers and what would happen and most likely did happen, was that they toddled off. How was I supposed to track them without eyes and why leave them here with all those things going bump in the night. How can I protect anyone against them, I ask you? Well, I'm not going to do the looking – can't, can I! Ask them strangers, maybe they took them. Look on that island for them, not about here. Scared to go over there, all of them and that Strongarm is the greatest coward of all. Taboo that island is and they can't cross there without me. That Strongarm discarded me like an old piece of bark, now he wants me to do a ceremony to render the island harmless so that they can go across and drive out those strange blackfellows. He should have done that before when that moma, that ghost was living there. Well, who cares, this place is peaceful and their problems are theirs, not mine. I'm just a blind old man who needs his peace and quiet.'

'And a bandicoot too and we all know about bandicoots and their lack of courage, don't we,' Jangamuttuk spoke up, stepping to the old man. Ludjee followed him.

'Well, I am a timid blind old man, so don't say "boo" and frighten me. As for bandicoots, they are great at digging out the roots and yams. If I was not my Dreaming animal, I would have long since starved. That mob of mine, except for my remaining wives, are useless. They talk about elders and respect, then let us fend for ourselves. Great blackfellows they are. Thank my Bandicoot ancestor for the tucker I get, but I do like a bit of red meat to mix with the veggies.'

'That can be done old man,' Jangamuttuk replied. 'And what is that you have buried in the ground. A spear and a good one at that. The point is sharp and well attached and the barbs face towards the haft. An excellent weapon, though on the light side. A kangaroo might drag it for miles, but it'll fly true. So Ludjee, my wife will stoke up the fire while I find you that red meat you crave.'

Carrying the spear across his shoulders, my father disappeared into the undergrowth and boulders which littered the bottom of the niche in the escarpment wall, while the old man continued to mumble on about his woes and Ludjee gathered wood to build up the fire. It had blazed up and sunk back to a heap of glowing coals by the time her husband returned with two wallabies on his shoulder. These he flung down, then taking up a piece of wood, he pushed aside the coals and scooped out a shallow hole in which to cook the carcasses. He pushed back the coals and Ludjee added more fuel. While they waited for the animals to roast, Jangamuttuk raised his voice to enter the old man's muttering.

'Well old fellow, last time you showed me that hole and it was down it that my son went. Now as far as I know, he's way under the ground and trapped there. Remember that night I was here? Your mind places tricks on you when you get old doesn't it; but no matter a good feed'll get the brain thinking and recalling. Soon we'll get stuck into those roasts and after you've feasted, I want you to show me another entrance. One that goes straight down.'

'He was human, wasn't he, and there is a rule that humans go that way. Well, are you and your wife human?'

'Not exactly, old fellow.'

'Well, you were the other night. You were that old blackfellow that came with a load of trouble for me. You killed that Strongarm's younger brother and he thinks I did it. Silly fool, but perhaps he'll treat me with some respect now.'

'Well, I'm not human now,' broke in my father changing to Goanna and waddling to him. The old fellow ran his hands over the rough skin and said: 'Naw, you certainly aren't what I would call human. Well then, those rules don't apply to you.'

Goanna changed back to Jangamuttuk and said: 'You can't have a thing like that for a brother. Strongarm should have realised that. I was only freeing him and his mob from a monster. Why, if it hadn't been for me, he might still be sipping from them whenever he felt thirsty.'

'Well, that's one monster less, but the one remaining is far worse,' Ludjee said. 'My son is down there with that evil female moma who is the cause of all our troubles. How I wish that I had put an end to the bitch when I had her at my mercy. A bitch she is, for she wants my dingo son.'

'Oh that one, told you last time she's a regular guest here. Comes fluttering around like some sort of moth or bat. Shook-shook-shook go her wings and this poor old blind fellow, he can't do a thing about it. He sits at his fire and he hears her land. Plop! And she comes softly creeping and her hands flutter over me and she whispers things that I never heard whispered before. Yes she does and if anyone took those kids it must've been her. Stupid woman, that silly wife of mine, never been right in the head and so she comes and drops her two sons here. They weren't even mine, but she left them here while she went off to some ceremony to which I wasn't even invited, let alone asked to officiate. Well, I had to get my vegetables and while I was collecting them, just adigging here and adigging there, some one or thing collected them. Come back, no kids. Can't hear them, can't feel them. Gone! Naturally, I'm getting the blame again. Can't do a thing right, you know.'

'Well old fellow take heart that the ceremony failed because of blood guilt. And your guest, she came and destroyed it almost causing a fight in the process. She killed another one of your mob too. She has to be stopped.'

'Well, it might have been her, but who knows, it might've been those blokes on the island. She's all right in her way. Got a mouth on her. Whispers about things that are awful and gloats over having done them. Must've been her, maybe ...'

'Enough of that evil thing and her dirty mouth,' Ludjee broke in with a shudder. 'The ghosts were bad; but this thing seems worse. It is a soul stealer and must be dealt with. And what is this blood guilt my husband keeps on prattling about. Those ghosts came to our country without permission. They went where they wished and took what they wanted, even women and children. That Malone on the island was one of them. He had my two sisters. Now he is dead as he well deserves. That moma has taken two infants and she must be destroyed, blood guilt or no blood guilt. We have to get after her, rescue those kids and find George and Wadawaka at the same time. So now that we have decided what to do, let's uncover those roasts and have a good feed.'

My father nodded at this and uncovered the wallaby and hacked them apart. He made sure that Milyado got the insides and placed his share on a platter of bark in front of him. The old fellow used what teeth remained to gnaw appreciatively at the meat and thrust his face into the stomach and sucked up the greens and pot liquor with gusto. At last he gave a huge burp, leant back against a convenient rock and declared: 'Lovely and tender and delicious. Now let us rest unto the evening. I am a bandicoot and the light of the day ill suits me. When the sun goes down, I will show you a special entrance which one of my ancestors left for only we bandicoot men to use. It is my secret and I wouldn't show any of my mob. They are only good for shouting and gesturing when they drive out an old blind man. Well, they will get nothing from me, but as you have fed me, then I will show you – though you must swear never to reveal it to anyone or thing. It will be our secret to share just as we have shared this wallaby.'

CHAPTER ELEVEN

That secret place is a long way from this god forsaken desert where the yellow nuggets make the living here the only thing worth the living for, if you get my meaning. I've been talking a blue streak and am beginning to trip over my words. Still there's a bit to go, but then the dark is holding up and daylight is hours away yet. So if you want to refill your mugs, I'll take a moment or two to recollect my thoughts, before I get my yarn moving again. Now, let me see, yes, far away, on this self same inland plateau which I'm told stretches from the west coast to the east coast, from the north to the south all dry and lonesome, well, close to the southern edge rose, and I guess it still does, a cone-shaped hill with a sharp serrated summit as if the top had been hacked off with a stone axe. There it was and what was strange about it that night was the three figures hovering over it. One was a goanna, another a manta ray and the third, a small brownish animal which as I picture that scene, flew down into the crater hidden by that serrated edge. Well, what else were we talking about but an extinct volcano and what does it have but passages leading down into the bowels of the earth. Keep that in mind and come with me to enter the underground.

'Follow me,' Bandicoot spoke within the minds of the other two Dreaming animals, for animals' throats and mouths are not made for human speech, and after this he darted into what appeared to be a cave set within the crater wall. It went in horizontally for a scant few metres to end at a stone wall. Goanna and Manta Ray reached the wall and looked around, then up and down. They saw an opening extending almost vertically down into the earth. Bandicoot had gone down this and they followed, fluttering down and down like leaves. The shaft seemed bottomless and soon they were in pitch blackness. Ludjee scraped against the side and regurgitated a crystal which shed a reddish light. All that it revealed were the smooth rock walls and the darkness below them. Down and down they floated, down and down, then the walls of the shaft began to glow with a myriad of luminescent specks. Ludjee stopped the light of her crystal and swallowed it. Below was a distant circle of whitish light. They fell through and out into a vast cavern. About them swirled a misty white illumination like clouds. They passed beneath this and below them spread the floor of the cavern, a great circular depression with promontories and indentations.

'There it is,' Bandicoot said in their minds. 'Somewhere below you, or in the tunnels leading from the cavern, you'll find what you are looking for; but I'm not going any further. The whole place scares me and it's too far underground for a bandicoot to enjoy. So goodbye and good luck for you'll need it. There are things here that'll make you shudder.'

He darted up towards the dark circle which was the entrance of the shaft while Goanna and Manta Ray hovered there indecisively, scoping out the lie of the land before resuming their descent. They landed on the hard packed floor of the cavern and resumed their human forms.

'It's a whole world down here,' Ludjee exclaimed, staring about. 'And it frightens me with a fear I have not known before.'

'It is indeed; but I have heard of this place. It is in some of our stories and they tell, as old Bandicoot just did, of things living down here that it is better to avoid,' Jangamuttuk replied. 'Still, it is a new world to that moma too and she will not have gone far into it. She should be lurking near and so should George and Wadawaka.'

'But, but I fear this place might be the end of us. To have suffered all that we have only to end up lost or imprisoned far underground. We are creatures of the day and of the overworld while she belongs down here where neither the sun nor moon rises to relieve the gloom and despair.'

'That boy needs me and then a shaman must make this trip', my father replied calmly in his usual manner. 'Put your fear aside, the island on which Fada imprisoned us was far worse and we were under the control of ghosts who began killing us off. And see, look at the floor, once it was part of Manta Ray's world.'

'So it was, though not now. There was an ocean here. There are shells underfoot. How I wish I was in that ocean, or any ocean with the water brushing against my sides as I hurtled along. I need the ocean, I need water,' she declared passionately. 'This place dries me and I feel my energy being drawn from my body.'

'It is but the effect of the rocky vault pressing down upon you,' Jangamuttuk stated, perhaps to reassure her and alleviate her fears. 'I am sure that there is water down here, perhaps vast pools of it and in them you can play; but that is not our purpose in being here. We are not explorers or seekers of hidden oceans, we have to search out our son and our chief mate and friend, Wadawaka. Now let us do that, but first let us mark out our escape route. Our exit is directly above the end of that promontory. Notice how it is shaped like a stone hammer.'

'I have a feeling that George is near, and that that is the place where we should look,' Ludjee replied, staring at the length of rocky wall that rose above them.

'They are both near and so is that monster. She radiates out her thoughts for all to pick up.'

'Mad thoughts too.'

'Strange that she who should be the most at home here, is the most distressed. No matter, I will go along the right side, you along the left and if we do not come across them along the rocky sides, we'll meet at the base of the promontory before we search further.'

'Be careful, be very careful, for there is danger here,' Ludjee answered with a shudder. 'It is as if someone is walking on my grave,' she cried, 'or that this is my grave.' She suddenly hugged her husband and clung to him as if she was loath to leave him.

'We'll be very careful, very, very careful but we must find them,' Jangamuttuk said with a sigh as he returned his wife's embrace. 'One is our only son and the other is our good friend who is needed if our voyage is to continue.'

'But you should not have sent our son,' my mother protested. 'He was too young.'

'It was the way it had to be,' my father replied. 'Just as it is the way it has to be for us. Now let us go and find them both.'

Ludjee detached herself reluctantly from her husband and began walking to her side of the promontory; but after a few steps she stopped for a last look at this man who had shared her life for so long. Mother and Father exchanged smiles, but there was a poignant sadness there as if it was for the last time. She watched his hand going to tug at his beard in the mannerism that she knew showed his disquiet and this was further emphasised when he began fiddling with his ochre-daubed ringlets. Then his hands dropped, he frowned and strode as briskly as his old bones would allow to his side of the promontory.

She was about to call to him that perhaps they should change into their Dreaming animal forms, when he disappeared from sight. With a long sigh, my mother walked to her side of the long rough wall of rock which had been indented and undermined by the ancient ocean. 'There indeed has been a sea,' she thought as she cursorily checked the rocks and holes for her son and once lover. She did this quickly, for she sensed that neither they nor that monster who held them in thrall were there.

The pitiless white light revealed everything, but nothing, for where the high wall of the promontory rose to her right, there was no living thing among the boulders or excavations that marked the rocky wall. Still, sometimes she started as if there indeed was something lurking there, for the light swirled and drifted a luminous mist with a hallucinatory effect. It was when she reached the base of the rocky wall that she heard a continuous murmuring like the buzzing of disturbed bees or wasps. She rounded an outcrop and the muttering became distinct words and from a female throat. As she went towards the voice, she heard it declare, 'A mother's work is never done'. Then she saw in front of her a grotto and entered it to find the naked white figure of the moma bent over a low platform on which lay two little blackfellows with their hands and legs moving like the feelers of insects.

'So you've become a mother,' she commented dryly. 'And as you know now, a mother's grief is never ending. You have my son down here just as you have these kids. None of them is yours,' she almost snarled, her mother's gaze staring at the flat white stomach bereft of stretch marks. 'A kidnapper, murderer and pervert, that's what you are. These kids must be returned to their parents.'

My mother felt she was in control of the situation, for the female thing before her was so white and puny in contrast to her own sturdy blackness; but she was deluding herself and she realised this when a sudden wave of rage and outrage came from the moma. She sprang directly at my mother who leaped to one side. Fully alert now, she kept her distance from the creature that whirled with her fingers curled into talons. 'Aha, I know you,' she screamed hysterically, her face contorting and her body trembling as she sought to control herself.

'Yes,' Ludjee replied, 'and I know you, but now I have no pity for you.'

'Well, don't, I want your fear not your pity,' snapped the moma. 'Here in my kingdom I am all powerful. A queen at the height of her power and in her own palace has little to fear from the likes of you. Stay and you shall be my servant.'

The two naked women, one black and robust the other slight and white, regarded each other warily.

My mother was a strong woman and did not remain overawed for long. She stepped forward and her bulk made the moma seem an even more slender girl. 'This is no place for kids or humans,' she declared. 'Without the sun and moon they will grow stunted. They need the free flow of air and the sky, not this rocky ceiling above them. This is your home and you are welcome to it; but these kids do not belong here, nor does my son. I want them.'

The moma bent over the two infants with a tender smile on her face: 'These are mine now. They have a loving mother and father. Above they would remain savages, here they will be princes. So beware, once you threatened me when I was but a callow girl, frightened in a strange land, now, here, I am a mature female and able to deal with you. You shan't have them. I won't let you take my precious darlings.'

'But these are not what I came for,' my mother retorted. 'There is my son who you drew down here. Him, I want as well as our captain, Wadawaka, who you have taken from us. Cast your mind back, once I told you to leave me and mine alone. You have not and ...'

'And, and, your dog came whining to me of his own accord. I took him in, for when these children grow they will need a pet and he is so faithful ...'

In spite of herself and in spite of knowing that the moma was more dangerous than before and ready to take her son away from her forever, she could not help feeling sorry for the creature. In a soft voice, my mother sought to get through to the thing which, after all, was female. 'I need my son back,' she murmured, 'and we all need Wadawaka, our chief mate and captain. You must understand that the needs of the living outweigh the needs of the dead. Please give them back to us. I as a mother implore you.'

'How can the undying be dead? Give back who or what to whom, when everything and everyone belongs to me here. You speak to a queen and she will not give up what is hers.'

'Live in your kingdom then, there are other subjects down here. Give back my son and my friend!'

'Your friend is now my lover and my husband. He is king down here along with his queen. He does not want to leave what he rules; and he is the father of these, my two children. See, they are as dark as he is.'

Ludjee, my mother, saw the madness that drove the moma on. Was there no reasoning with this thing? All she could do was keep her occupied until her husband came up and together they would deal with her; but where was he? Jangamuttuk should have been here by now. Perhaps, he had been affected by the swirling light. She was sure that the underground with its strange restless illumination and the stale flatness of air had driven this creature into madness and hallucination and if this could happen to a thing of darkness, what might it do to four beings that loved the light? 'Jangamuttuk, Jangamuttuk,' she called softly to herself, hoping that he might hear her in his mind; but there was no indication that he heard. With a sigh she turned her attention back to the crazy thing before her.

'Yes,' she said, keeping her voice calm and soothing, 'but I see that these little ones are not babies, but infants. No longer crawling ones, they totter on their two legs. I am a mother and have been through the birthing process more than once. It takes ten passes of the moon to create a baby, then another twelve passes to pull them to their feet. They have a grieving mother above this place who suffered as she birthed them. Just think how sad she feels.'

The moma gazed down lovingly at the two infants and replied: 'They are mine and his. How can I give them up? They are a sign of our true love.'

Ludjee could not help herself and rolled her eyes. What might she say to this deluded creature? Again, she looked around for her husband. What had happened to him? 'Well, these are not my concern,' she said again in a soothing voice, 'but I am down here to see my son and our friend. I want to know how they fare and if they need anything.'

'They need nothing from you. Treat them as the dead who are lost to you forever.'

'They are alive and I must see them. Please let me see them.'

'No, no, I need them more than you do. I must have them with me! Once I had a dark lord and he took what he wanted and deserted me. I, a simple girl, had to learn how to survive alone in a hostile world. A solitary night creature without family or friends, every hand was lifted against me. Do you know how it is to be a pale thing haunting the darkness, seeking and finding prey but never companionship. Well, I am beyond that now and have found a companion. Wadawaka is mine and as for your son, he is my dog. What else need you know, now go! They wish to be with me, even though they do not have my blood on their mouths – though when they desire to pass beyond the human, I will gift them eternal life. Never to grow old is a gift beyond all gifts.'

'Or blood guilt with a sentence of eternal damnation.'

The creature snarled and was about to spring at my mother when one of the infants mewed plaintively and stretched out his tiny arms. Instantly, the moma swept both of them up in her arms, exclaiming as she did so: 'See, that is a child's love for his mother. See, how they feed from my body.'

'You are a milkless thing and have turned them to blood suckers. You have made them yours. Psha, how rancid they smell!'

'What, they smell as sweetly as other babes. Taken away from their savage – no, I am a good mother and know how to care for them, my sweet darlings who feed from my life's blood. Come and see how tenderly I bathe them,' she smiled, sweeping past my mother and out into the cavern.

Ludjee went after her, for Jangamuttuk must be at the base of the promontory by now. He was not there and she worried even more as she followed after the moma. They entered an area filled with numerous pools of water, above some of which the silvery mist gently moved. Out in the open or main body of the cavern, my mother's eyes darted about and she consoled herself with the thought that her husband had found her son and Wadawaka. Now all she had to do was distract the creature until she received the signal to escape from this wretched place and this awful creature.

'Ah, yes, these pools are warm and sometimes hot,' the moma said as she put the toddlers gently down upon the ground. She took their hands and led them towards a crevice filled with water which steamed.

'This one should do nicely,' she exclaimed, glancing slyly at my mother.

'But it seems too hot. I can feel the heat coming off it from here,' Ludjee protested, her mother instincts aroused.

'No, it is barely warm to the touch,' the creature replied with a strange smile. She let go the hands of the children and thrust her fingers into the steaming water. 'There, feel it yourself, if you don't believe me.'

My mother did not move. She thought that it might be some trick, though what, she could not guess.

The moma dipped her fingers into the water again, then said: 'Perhaps you are right. It may be too hot for their tender skins. Check it for me, will you. That vapour you see above the surface is but escaping gas. Smell it, it stinks.'

She stepped back, giving my mother enough room so that she might feel safe to come and sample the water. 'It is far too hot,' Ludjee exclaimed, kneeling down at the ledge of the pool.

'Of course it is, you fool,' the moma screamed, leaping forward and flinging her weight against the back of the kneeling woman. My poor mother. She felt herself being propelled out and down into the boiling water. She didn't even have time to cry out as she plunged beneath the surface.

'There sample that,' the female thing cried. 'There, experience what happens to those who seek to deprive me of those who are mine.'

Now she in turn knelt at the edge of the pool to watch my mother's struggle to survive. Her head thrust up and she gave a heart-rending scream that turned into a gurgle as the moma thrust her under again. She sought to change to Manta Ray to escape, but on leaping up, found that she could not fly. Again the monster's hands grabbed her and held her under, then she disappeared into the depths of the pool and was seen no more.

'I am a thing of the cold and heat cannot harm me,' the moma shrieked, her madness taking control of her. She picked up the two kids and whirled them about in a frenzied dance as she chanted: 'Cook well, cook well, my friend. Boil your flesh; how tender it is. My dog will feast, will feast on his mother's bones. He lacks red meat and now he has it. Where is my dog! Gnaw on the bones, crack them open and get at the marrow. A mother's body is sweet and tender. Come, children, let us find your father and our dog. Both of them can enjoy the meat.'

CHAPTER TWELVE

Now my remembrance of things past was becoming hazy, affected by the shifting mists of light. Where was I and what was I doing here? I had some vague recollection that I had gone underground on some sort of quest or rescue mission which seemed silly. Oh, yes, to believe that would be to believe that I could fly. I was a doggy and well looked after by a loving mistress. I was her pet and just a whiff of her scent made me wag my tail furiously. My joy had become complete when I became reunited with my friend, Wadawaka.

Now in my new home, everything was perfect, or it should have been; but the white light swirled about me, evoking strange phantom shapes, so much so that I became a very confused doggy and the stress changed my body odour so that I could hardly identify myself. There was a stink of fear emanating from me and this mixed with the dead smells of the underground to make me really nervous. I desperately wished to get my nose into more natural smells. Here every smell, including those of my friends, or should I say my loved ones, merged with the overall stench of decay and dissolution. I needed other smells and sights about me, the familiar multitudes of the world above teeming with life and roofed by the glimmering stars. When I raised my snout and sniffed, I imagined that I could smell the smoke from those far-off fires, the slight burning odour of something which was not wood, but which was as familiar as the smoky eucalyptus scent of my father, Jangamuttuk.

But then, but then, what was I doing here? I felt so divorced from my mob and my country. I felt so alone; but I was with my friend and with my mistress so how could I feel isolated and abandoned? I was indeed a confused young doggy and I gave a low moan and settled down with my snout on the ground and my eyes staring up. I lay there thinking things over and considering that even my mistress had changed.

I wished that she had remained as I remembered her from our first meeting, slightly mocking but kind at the same time. Once, when she touched me, a wild ecstasy surged up in me; but now, although I was overjoyed to be with her again, I sensed a savagery in her which made me cower. Her mind shattered and spumed as if under attack from a furious tempest and when my thoughts merged with hers, it was a terrifying experience. My humanity whispered in my doggy mind that she was quite mad, but I would never believe that about my loving mistress. She was just a bit upset and would calm down sooner or later. After all, she had my friend with her as well as her dog.

Still, all this thinking was not good for my doggy mind and I whimpered as I kept my eyes on my friend, begging him for a pat; but he, too, was not his own true self. There was little warmth and affection from this man who seemed to have his consciousness hidden underneath a thick stifling blanket through which few emotions could pass. Where he was once active and a bundle of energy, he was now passive and detached. I got up slowly, shook myself and wandered over to him. I pressed against his leg; I needed to be stroked, but he paid me no heed and went off to his rows of fungi and began to align each mushroom. Each one was spaced precisely the same distance apart in rows, in a soil which smelled only of mustiness and rank things. If only I could summon up my strength, I would play the bad dog and mess up his garden; but instead I flopped down and lay there watching him shift a mushroom a minuscule distance from another.

He emitted a low keening as he worked, then stopped and began murmuring to himself: 'There was that place in which I found myself. It had a swirling whiteness too, but the whiteness of that place was salt and it stung my body, not my mind as this mistiness does. I have a half barrel in the slush beside me and a shovel in my hand and I scoop up the whiteness into the barrel, empty it onto a growing pile of bitter glowing whiteness, then do the same again. Over and over again. We slave on, the sun blazing down on our heads like a bonfire. My body blisters from the heat and the crystals cake on my skin. My feet from constantly being in the slush are full of dreadful abscesses, cankers that eat down to the very bone. If you look you will see the scars, where the whiteness etched into my black skin. Still, what was the physical pain compared to the mental. I never knew my mother and once, on a Sunday when we were allowed to rest or remain away from the salt, a sloop came into the port and I carried aboard the salt and among the black people they had condemned to work alongside me I thought I saw my mother. I called, "Mammy, mammy", and ran to her, ran to her though I was a fully grown man; but whether she was my mother or not, I know not to this day, for I was driven back to carry on the whiteness and when I returned and managed to speak to her, I found that the poor woman was insane and all that she could do was babble on. There was no sense in her. It is like that here. There's much talking and little sense. I too babble on like that poor woman and if I do not babble I sing and if I do not sing or babble, I remain silent, and one or other or all three are the same foolishness. I need the rough meaningful voice of the sea that speaks of storms and tempests; the abruptness of the waves and even that smell of salt which once I dreaded as it ate into my flesh and marked my skin with whiteness ...'

And he bent his dreadlocked head over his tidy rows of mushrooms and began to rearrange them feverishly into tidy pale rows, while I lay flattened on the ground. Then, my hackles rose in sheer terror as into my mind came a dreadful single shriek from a stout black woman as she fell into a boiling pool of water. I should have known her and did, but my mind was not my own and it was filled with my mistress screaming on and on in triumph as she stared down into a pool where something neither human nor fish writhed before sinking beneath the bubbling surface. Even though I was terrified by the scene and by my mistress's behaviour, I had not eaten for what seemed many days, so I began salivating as I smelled the odour of boiling flesh. And my mistress's voice urged me to the feast. I left my friend to his mushrooms and trotted off in her direction, her voice calling me to her, before she began babbling of other things in which I had little interest.

'He is my man and here I have made a home for him. What more can I do for one who roamed the world homeless until he came to me. I felt his lack and so brought him to this refuge. Now we are together and will remain together deep within the bowels of the earth where I need never face the full burning of that sun. Away from the threat of that eye, I can exult in my full strength and power and destroy those who torment me with their demands. No one can separate us! We are a family, for I have given him children and now he has a dog to keep him company while I look after my little ones. Such a loving family we are. No one dare separate us! Such an evil crime and one which needs swift vengeance. Once I was secure in the bosom of my family, though I must admit I longed to be free of it; but then it was unlike this, my new family in which I am safe and secure. Yes, safe and secure!'

And I came to her while her voice stopped, then whined on again. 'I will build up this underworld to rival the one above,' she threatened. 'Now I have my dark lord at my side and we need no other, only underlings to do our bidding. Yes, he is with me and when he turns to me by his own free will, then we will be as one being in two bodies. Side by side, we will ride the upwards air currents to the warm world where he and I shall hunt together. Soon, yes, I see this already, for he longs for the stars and the moon, and who can give them to him, but me. Together in the darkness we shall roam the world and when we have gorged ourselves to repletion, we shall return to our dark kingdom to rule without fear of revolt.'

Then her voice stuttered to a halt and I saw a dark figure come to her, an old man with matted grey locks smeared with red ochre and a grey beard merging with the misty light so that he seemed bereft of the lower portion of his face, except for the darkness of a mouth with worn down stained teeth, from between the gaps of which his voice emerged, grating forth in sadness and grief: 'What you have done, you have done, but I still want my boy, your supposed pet, and also Wadawaka my adopted kin. Our blood guilt has been satisfied and so now is the time for me to reclaim my own. You, you belong down here in this underground where the shades of the dead mingle their blank despair with your fancies to make you mad.'

Confused, for a long moment I stared at the slim white body of my mistress, glowing and free from all scars, then at the naked old black man who stood bowed by age and with the cicatrices of his manhood across his chest. It was my father! I gave a yelp and bounded to his side. Thank the ancestors, he had come for me. I was tired of this sorry place and wanted to be at the helm of the schooner with his songs driving us to the west.

Then my mistress gave a scream of pure rage which flung me into a turmoil. Again, I was a very confused doggy and could only watch as she bounded forward. My father, a victor of many a martial contest, merely skipped aside and she rushed past him before she could stop. She turned a white face with gleaming fangs at him and shrieked: 'I know you, you old savage and if we are to talk of shades, well, there is a new one here and a place for another.'

Jangamuttuk, my father, did not shout back, but replied in his calm voice – which now held a trace of sadness in it as well – and with an authority which halted her as she prepared to spring at him again. She looked like an albino wallaby, frozen in an instant before the heavy spear struck her down. 'Stay there!' my father ordered. 'I know you and your kind, keep well away from me. I have means to subdue you.'

He succeeded in quietening the creature whom I still regarded as my mistress. I hoped that he wouldn't hurt her, or that she wouldn't hurt him, for I loved them both. As he finished speaking I sensed a quaver in his voice which showed that he was wavering in his determination and power. My mistress noticed it too and changed her tactics. By an effort of will she pushed down the delirium which trembled her body and made her a wild thing. She now stood before my father, like a young girl who was afraid of the irascibility of an older, but still virile, male.

'Please, please,' she said, speaking in a soft, caressing voice which was that of a daughter or a young wife whose only fault was overweening love. 'Please,' she said again, then went on to defend herself. 'I have done no wrong, except to claim a husband. Is that wrong for a young woman to do?'

Her voice was so alluring, that my tail began wagging and I felt like rolling over on my back to have my belly stroked. It was at last her old voice, filled with love and kindness. My father was not taken in and did not relax his stance or words. 'They are to return with me,' he said again with quiet authority, but still with that quaver which betrayed a certain weakness. It was this that made me go to him and be rewarded with a rough hand tugging at my ears. Now we both faced her, man and his dog, or rather father and son.

'Well, my dog certainly likes you,' she replied with a delicate shrug that set her small pert breasts shifting. 'Well, you may borrow him, but as for my husband. He and I belong together and if you wish to take him you must have me too.'

'No, that can never be, for it is from such as you that we are fleeing. We have no need of you and then, I know what you would do to us. We do not want to be your caitiffs to do with as you wish.'

My mistress now looked determined, but still sweet and attractive, even jerking her chin up as she pouted, then exclaimed: 'But there is a higher voice which says, what God has joined together, let no man tear asunder. It is what we have been taught; but you – as a savage – do not have laws like this. You couple like animals.'

'Savages? And what savages we are to be the victims of such barbarians who believed such words, but still raped and plundered who and what they wanted. Not even young boys were safe from them, so it is best not to mention what happened to our young girls and women. We too have a law, which is let no man take from us what the ancestors have given. So what you have taken, must be returned. This is my son, and Wadawaka, our chief mate, our captain and our adopted kinsman, was sent to us by our ancestors. Before he came to us, he was in agony, and now with you that suffering has returned. Give him up so that he may be healed.'

The girl before us now stamped her foot in exasperation and her expression changed. She gave up the pretense and it was now the moma that confronted my father and me. 'Your laws are worthless. The savage has none but his own demons to obey so let him beware!'

'I am, but I am the Master of the Ghost Dreaming and am frightened of no such thing as yourself.'

'Enough, enough,' she replied, her voice becoming shrill. 'We are a family and he is the father of my two precious ones. Now go or be destroyed.'

'Enough of these, your moma fantasies. Things like you fall easily into such imaginings. All you have are the dregs of a past life and you seek to reconstruct them in this underground filled with the phantoms of the dead. Those children, there is not the hint of whiteness about them. You stole them from above and couldn't even keep them whole. You perverted them as soon as you felt the need arise. Now you have deprived them of their growing. They are lost to the world above.'

'Deprived them, deprived them,' my mistress screamed, her control completely gone. 'Well, I can deprive you of the remainder of your worthless life, you old fool. Your meandering songs may cause animals to prick up their ears and ghosts to flee, but they are gibberish to me. Both my husband and myself are impossible to quell. Know you that he was called the Black Englishman and feted wherever he went in my homeland. He but plays the savage where you are the savage. Reconcile yourself to his loss, for he has resumed his rightful place. Now I've had enough of your senile prattlings. Get back to your tribe and control those fools with broken words and sleight of hand tricks. My husband has had enough of you and yours, he is here with me by his own choice. He has chosen freely.'

'But what is freedom of choice where you are concerned,' my father replied as calmly as he could, for I could not help but think that in contrast to the vibrancy of my mistress, he indeed looked like a senile old man. I felt a deep sadness for him and remained at his side as his words trailed away. 'You met my wife, Ludjee, and found her blood not to your liking. Wadawaka's blood also is poisonous to you. You will not be able to turn him. He was born on the sea and there is no earth in him.'

'Well, her blood was poisonous indeed; but why not try her flesh. It should be well cooked by now and falling off the bone. My dog will love her when he gets his teeth into her and you are more than welcome to join in the feast.'

I had never seen my father look so pitiful and weak. 'What is this you seek to do with me?' he asked in a quavering voice from which all authority had gone. I nuzzled at his hand in commiseration and he pulled at my neck hair with a hand that was anything but weak, though his voice belied this. 'Let us go, is all I ask,' he whispered. 'We will not harm you.'

'And yet, and yet, you seek to destroy my family.'

'Well, those children, they are yours; but let me have my son. I have no-one to look after me in my old age,' he cried.

'All who are down here are mine, my dog, my husband and my children. Now go!'

'Not without my son. Please, not without him.'

'You have no son, you old fool. This dog is my pet and will stay with me. Now go! I am tired of this charade. If you have tears to shed, prepare to shed them, for you get nothing from me. Leave me and mine alone. I learnt that phrase from your once wife, so be it. Now get!'

I couldn't help thinking, for so much was I under the influence of that female thing, that the old were tiresome, for my father refused to leave us. I wanted him to go, for I drooled in anticipation of the meat she had promised me. Now he displayed a senile anger that fooled no-one. Poor father, I really did feel sorry for him as he sobbed out: 'Enough of this, enough, enough. George is my only son. He is not stolen property. If I had my spear I would drive the wooden point deep within that white heart of yours and watch in glee the stolen blood gush forth.'

'Now, now, old man,' she replied, gloating, 'stop your yelling. See where my babies sleep. Do not disturb them, for they are hungry little things and might find you to their liking.'

My father gave a deep sigh and stared at the moma; no, no she was my mistress. She was a small white thing that stood before him, but I felt the power within her and I'm sure my father did too. In spite of her slight form, she now seemed to tower over him and tendrils of white mist curled around her as she gave a strange shrill of a laugh that thrilled me through and through. 'You are finished old man, stay or go, but if you continue to pester me, I'll call my husband to put a stop to it. He will, he will ...' And strangely, at the thought of Wadawaka, her control broke and she rushed away with thoughts so scrambled that they repelled me. I became terrified of her yet again, and pressed closer to my old father who suddenly chuckled.

'Moma are crazy. Keep them talking long enough and give them an emotional jolt every now and again, and sooner rather than later they break down. Silly thing, she has rushed off after Wadawaka because she can never rule him and must keep him under her control at all times. Well, I'll soon put an end to her. I have a ceremony that will bind her. I do not want to kill her, merely render her helpless while we escape. But there's something evil that she has done and she used it to play with my mind. She almost had me for a second.' And he chuckled again then told me to change back to my human form.

I tried to, but couldn't. The effort made my hair stand on end, but still I remained Dingo. My father smoothed my hair down, chewed thoughtfully on his beard, then left the grotto with me trotting at his side. Then, I felt my mistress calling to me and there arose that familiar longing of wanting to be with her. I hung back and she called, promising me entry to the feast she was preparing. Yes, I longed for that red meat, but the thought of it pulled a sadness from the deep recesses of my mind and this merged with the grief coming from my father. We were entering that state of mourning which came when someone dear had departed; but though I tried I could not recall who that was, especially when I was starving and needed that feed of rich red meat.

CHAPTER THIRTEEN

There was a foreboding atmosphere in the cavern as I padded along beside my father unwilling to leave him. I sensed that another awful thing was about to happen. I felt that the tendrils of whitish mist which had begun to drift about might coalesce into a lightning bolt to strike me down. This would at least put an end to my hunger which was so great that it threatened to send me off to my mistress even though her calling had stopped.

Jangamuttuk hunted about and found two large pebbles. He struck them together, was satisfied with the sound they made and hit them together again. The sharp clack-clack travelled out and returned in a myriad of echoes to confound my ears. They reverberated throughout the cavern, striking the walls and returning in diminishing potencies. I lifted my snout and watched my father clashing the stones together until the clacking filled the whole underground. My ears twitched, then my nose and finally my whole skin. I quivered with the rhythm and it lifted me up and deposited me beside a limpid pool redolent with the aroma of freshly cooked meat. How delicious it smelled. I lowered my snout over the water, letting drops of saliva fall into it as I snatched up strips of boiled flesh and gulped them down. I fed on and on and then ended my meal with a long drink of sweet water. How sated I felt and it was then that the rhythm stopped and I found myself just a short distance from my father. It had all been an hallucination and I growled in disappointment. I found the scent of Wadawaka and followed it back to him. At least he had fish.

He was still at his patch of fungi, arranging and rearranging the straight rows of mushrooms. I had had enough of his compulsive behaviour and galloped through his garden before making it back to my father and nipping at his leg. His loud clacking had broken one of the stones and he was looking about for another of the right size and shape. He found one, picked it up, hit it, listened to the clack, nodded his head, then decided that he would follow his dog of a son back to where our mate was. The wrecking of his garden seemed to have broken the spell he had been under, for as we closed in on him he stared at us, though still somewhat blankly.

Jangamuttuk walked about him, examining both him and his garden. He muttered something about him having been sung, then began his clacking again. It reverberated backwards and forwards, a complex rhythm overawing the song he began to sing in a high thin voice so unlike his usual gruff chanting.

She made of him
A ghost down under
Way down under
While she plunders
Us of blood so red

Tip this place asunder
Asunder rip the witch
Asunder blunder plunder
The rock is hard
Way down under.

His voice choked off. He went dumb and this caused me to glance up into his face. It was twisted in a peculiar expression and his eyes shone with unshed tears. He dropped one of his pebbles to fiddle with his beard nervously, then bent down, stroked my head and tweaked my ears while he murmured: 'It is too far, too far under, and too, too late.' He flung his other pebble hard at the rocky floor and it shattered into a thousand pieces with a harsh sound that startled Wadawaka into awareness of himself. I saw the light of recognition flicker in his eyes and strengthen when my father went to him and embraced him.

'Come to your senses,' he shouted. 'You were born on the sea and meant for the sea, not the land. No, and it is your job to lead them west. Forget this underground, for the waters long have receded from it. Forget her too, if you can, and we too can.'

'Long receded,' the seaman replied, staring out across the bed of the dried up sea, 'but perhaps it has drained into the middling earth. If I explored this place I could find it. Might it not be my goal, your goal, our goal ...?' He broke off in confusion and stared down at where I had wrecked his neat rows of fungi. 'My garden needs to be put to rights. Some animal has been at it. The mushrooms were just about ready to harvest too. I can make a fine chowder with them and so delicious that it will tempt my wife to eat, for she has forsaken food as have my little ones, but they are still too young for solids. They cling to their mother's breasts.'

'Silly bugger,' commented my father dryly. 'It's these so-called mushrooms that keep you under her spell. Well, find your mind and cast it back. Fada had us planting such things too. They affected us so much that he had us singing *Onward Christian Soldiers*. Find your mind and stop cultivating those things. You are Wadawaka, Seaborn, and without a wife and kids. All you have is us and we have you. Remember, lead them west!'

'I have always been in two minds,' Wadawaka replied slowly, bending down and pulling up a mushroom which he seemed about to eat. Instead, he flung it from him and went on: 'A woman is like a blanket. When you cover yourself with it, it is itchy, but if you put it aside you feel cold. It is really like that, or once love bitten always smitten.'

'Yes, and a man with deepset eyes cannot see the new moon as you cannot see the snake in your belly. Be aware and leave her to sleep alone in the fastnesses of the earth. Unlike a blanket, she'll give you no warmth.'

'But it is warm down here. That dog needs food. Hear the rumbling of his empty belly. There is fish, ocean fish that have been trapped down here for so long that they lack the eyes to see. They huddle in the pools and I can catch them with my bare hands. I place them in the hot pools which serve as cooking pots. Lift your nose and smell, that is a fish cooking. It will be succulent and the flesh will be firm. The dog can quieten his belly ...'

But the cooking flesh did not smell like fish and as my father sniffed his face collapsed into his beard. He seemed to shrink within himself; but I didn't know what was the matter with him. Flesh I wanted; fish I could do without!

'Too much illusion here,' my father groaned. 'Too much for this old man who is beginning to lose his way. I have to get out! We all have to, for the light swirls about and what our senses sense belongs only to this underground.'

'Leave, leave,' Wadawaka murmured. 'Leave for what. I have a wife and children and here I am at peace. Here I shall stay where once the ocean waves clashed. You go back to your mob, they need you. Take the dog, he'll guide you to where the canoe awaits. Give the Ferryman some fish and he'll take you.'

'Enough of this stupidity,' my father shouted in exasperation. 'It is this place that twists our reality. It is she who seeks to control us. You are Leopard, become him and break her spell.'

'Leopard, Leopard, yes, I remember, and is the woman of that story the queen of this underground? Once, yes in my mother's country, there lived in such a place as this a woman who was wise and could control the weather. Her skin was as white as the clouds above and she lived only on a plant with a spiky fruit. It was all she ate. And it is said that she was married, married not to a leopard, but to a huge snake who lived deep in the depths of the earth and came to her when the light faltered in the mouth of the cave. She was what we call a *mangu,* a witch. One night there appeared a flame on the ridge above her cave and it was a leopard. He glowed, spotted all over with the rays of the sun. He waited for the snake to come to her, for the powers of that mangu came from the serpent which entered her body and spoke through her mouth about hidden and secret things. Leopard waited on the hill top and when that snake entered the witch, he bounded down and swallowed both up. Now that leopard had the woman in his belly and that woman had the snake in hers and he could dream the future from them; but when he did, he found that it was all bad for Africa, so no good came to that leopard from learning how to divine the future.'

'Enough of stories!' My father erupted into an anger I had seldom seen from him. 'This female thing is as bad as the ghosts that ravished our land and people. She is not a woman to be loved, just as this place is not for living things. It is the land of the dead inhabited by those who have lost their way. I am a shaman and know this as fact. I would conduct a ceremony to release these souls that flutter about us like moths as they seek the route to the skyworld; but alas, my voice falters and down here my songs have little potency. Come, let us leave this place and seek the free sky. Enough of mangu, witches and their evil ways.'

'Enough of old men and their senile ways,' Wadawaka's wife screamed, rushing to us and standing next to her mate.

Now I stared at these two and it was as if the light of day stood next to the black of night. They held each other's gaze and there was a bond between them, different from what was between us, either as friend or pet. Jealousy made me leave the old man, my father, and go to sit beside my mistress. Such was love and I might be rewarded. I was, but not with what I wanted, instead she smiled down at me and scratched my head, as with her other hand she took that of Wadawaka.

'See, how happy we are together,' she laughed viciously at the old man who I had known before.

The poor old chap. I felt sorry for him and wondered why he did not join us. We could all be happy down here as long as I got enough food, though not that fish!

The old man began to sing:

> *The sea murmurs in your blood*
> *Blood bereft of the thickness of earth*
> *Flow on, roll on, wave after wave.*

It broke our mood of oneness. Wadawaka's hand fell away from that of the female. He stared at her with hostility as he said: 'You, I have met before and let you live, though I knew that you could be dangerous. So much for pity!'

'So you remember Amelia do you and what you did to her. Well, remember her for what she has done to you. Made you a king and given you a kingdom.'

'And such a kingdom. It reeks of dead flesh.'

'Does it matter, for when you came to me you smelt of the fish stinking ocean. Now, you smell but of the earth.'

'Well, better the ocean with spray dashing in my face than this evil place of death. There is no movement here.'

'And yet you came here willingly, for only those who wish to enter, may; and you made your choice when you took me, and in the taking inherited this world. I can never forget those promises you made to me ...'

'What promises, I remember that you attacked me and got more than you expected.'

'And so did you, you ungrateful cur. At least my dog loves me with an unfailing love, but you ... This old black savage comes in his senility prattling who knows what to you and you are ready to desert both wife and children. Well, what is there for you above? Answer me that! Just more like him and a stolen schooner that invites the hangman's noose. Piracy, sir, you'll swing from the yardarm. They have no mercy for such as you.'

'What, to be trapped here. Up there, if the sea is denied me, there is the sky and the tug of air at my pelt.'

'Pelt indeed, you are not an animal, though you pretend to be. What need of others, pray, when you can fly with me and hunt such animals as that old man.'

It was then that Jangamuttuk suddenly broke away from his despondency with a half assumed chuckle that rang false. 'He has a different future beyond this pit. He knows it and so do you and I. Let's finish off our little conversation and be on our way.'

I, too, had had enough of this endless talk and was sick of this light and this cavern. I wanted to pull down a wallaby and get my snout into its innards. But still they had not done.

'Old man, stop your mouth or you'll have another mouth which will gurgle as your life blood gushes forth. He is my mate and the father of my children.'

'Semblance only. A mad wish which you have inflicted on yourself and on him. This underground is made for the craziness such as that you project. We have been taken in by it and now are emerging to bid you adieu.'

'Old man, you may have powers beyond this place, but here you struggle while I exult. Far from the sun, he and I shall remain.'

But Wadawaka sidled away from the female and with him I came. At last, he was himself. His hand came down and stroked my back, found a prickle from the overground and pulled it out. He held it up to his eyes as he declared in a voice which grew in strength as he went on: 'I am tired of this eternal evening. I want the full light of the day, the full change of the seasons and the wild gale battering at my vessel as I seek to control her.'

'You shall have it; you shall; you shall, just stay with me and I will give you that and more,' the female wailed, beside herself. She knew that she had lost us, but then I was still her friend and wanted her hand on me as well as some of that meat ...

'We are going.'

'But your children, poor fatherless mites.'

'I and you have little in common, certainly not children.'

'We have the hangman in common if we are caught, and if you leave, my vengeance follows. I am not a thing to be mocked and flung aside.'

'And yet you are, for I discarded you once before. Now, I've had enough of your rantings.'

Wadawaka turned with us and we were about to walk off and leave the female behind when I felt her calling me to her.

'You cannot go, just like that. Stay here. I promise not to hurt you and I have even returned to you your powers. Stay, there is a whole world down here with tunnels reaching beyond your imagination. Stay, I am not a woman to begrudge a husband friends. Dog, come with me while they decide.'

She left us standing there with her appeal lingering in my mind. Suddenly it was imperative and, unable to resist, I went off after her, continuing on even when her diseased mind became harsh with threats.

'They think females are weak and defenseless, to be discarded or taken at their male whim. Well, they'll soon realise that I am not to be crossed and wherever he goes, I will follow, not because I love him but because I will it. I have an eternity to fill and I am amused enough by him to let him occupy a few years of my time. Such will be my revenge. He will realise that I am not a toy to be discarded and flung away. Let them talk and if they seek to escape, that'll be the end of the old man and as for my dark lord, I will let him live for the time being. He is my husband after all and a woman fights for what is hers, and when losing exacts a bloody revenge.'

CHAPTER FOURTEEN

'When I was a child my mother used to tell us this story, this ancient tale to me, Amelia, and my sister Eliza. Then it had little meaning for me, but now I suppose it has; why else should I remember it? Perhaps my mother also repeated this story to us because she was seeking to reveal to us what hidden powers of vengeance lie within the female. Be that as it may, her story comes to me now when I am suffering beyond relief.

'Long, long ago in ancient Greece this fair princess left all for the love of a man named Jason. He came to her for help and she helped him, even to the extent of killing her very own brother. She rescued him from certain death and Jason, swearing eternal fealty, took her back to his native land. There her help did not cease, for she had the powers of a witch and with these she even saved his old father's life and it was all for him. For nine nights she had to go out into the pitch blackness to gather the necessary herbs. When she had done this, she set up two altars to the goddesses, Hecate of the Underground and Hebe who knew the ways of herbs and potions. After this she got the old man to the altars and cut his throat so that his blood flowed over them and into the open mouths of the goddesses. When his veins were empty she refilled them with the liquid she had distilled from the herbs. He lived, and others came to her for such life as she might give and the goddesses were happy with their supply of blood; but then she rashly allowed one of her patients who had offended her to die and had to flee with her husband, Jason, to another city where he was made welcome, but she was not. He was received with such warmth that the king of that city offered him his daughter in marriage. Jason eagerly accepted, deciding to abandon she who had done so much for him. Medea, for such was the wronged wife's name, was filled with rage and planned a terrible revenge on her husband and her rival. She destroyed the girl by sending her a beautiful robe and a bejewelled crown. The princess was delighted and put them on. The robe clung to her skin and burnt away her flesh to the very bone and the crown ate into her skull with living fire. Now came the revenge on her unfaithful husband. The wronged woman took her own two sweet babes and cut their throats. She let that tender young blood flow across the bed she and that ungrateful man had shared as wife and husband. Such was her vengeance and when it was finished with she called on Hecate and Hebe to take her away and they did.

'That was how my mother told the gory tale to we two tykes who lapped up the words with our mother's milk. And now I tell it to you two little kids, though there shall be a different ending in this reality.' So finished off my mistress as she fondly regarded the babies lying wide-eyed on their platform of soft moss.

She picked the infants up, holding them away from her breasts as they attempted to sup. She stared at each tiny face as she murmured: 'How could a mother kill such little ones, but if one woman has done so, can another be far behind? Vengeance does not only belong to the ancient Medea, the daughter of a god, it belongs also to me, one of the Undying and thus a true companion to Hebe and Hecate.'

Now she pressed the two black kids to her breasts, then again held them away before they could lacerate her breasts. She saw then how grimy and rank they were with dried blood. 'Such poor things,' she said, pulling a face as if they repelled her. 'They have the look of their father about them and I declare that there is not much of me in them at all. Why should it be me who looks after them when it is he who has disowned them? Their father, he should be here to tend to their needs. See how grubby they are. They need to be scrubbed down to their bare bones. Poor, poor orphans. Come, dears, let us go to that pool where I and your father spent many a happy hour, frolicking in the warm water and so often making such, sweet sweet love that it was scarcely endurable even for one as I and for him too of course, the ingrate, for I saw how his eyes turned up in the uttermost ecstasy and after, how completely spent he sank into slumber. How he loved me then.'

She sighed and her unsteady eyes flitted about the grotto. 'This was a goodly place, is a goodly place, far from the heavy rays of the sun which threaten me with extinction. My husband says that it is always evening here and so it is an eternal evening just at the close of day when the beautiful night waits ready to pounce upon what remains of the light. How peaceful and content were we in our home, I busy with my infants, and he tending his garden; but it was too good to last. Those two strangers, so-called adopted kin came to upset him. They destroyed his love for me and for that they will pay as will he. Now, my little ones, don't wriggle so in my arms. Just wait, in a moment I'll set you down into that nice pool where you can splash about.'

I was following along behind her and crept to the edge of the pool she was making for. I lowered my nose to taste the water, but jerked it back just in time. It was hot, too hot for drinking. I whimpered suddenly as emotions washed over me. I knew that I was not really a dog, but a human who wanted to have the scent of his own kind about him. How I missed my mother. I wondered where she was, and why when I thought of her I was overwhelmed by a deep sense of loss. I listened to the female I was with babble on about faithless fathers and orphaned children while I thought of being with Ludjee and how she would sometimes shout at me, then fiercely give me a hug that revealed her love for me.

Suddenly, the female shrieked and screamed out, 'No father; no father! What use are these things for me! No husband, no husband. I see his mind and he will leave me alone within these vast caverns and endless tunnels. Well, never, never, shall it be: where he goes, I go.'

I whined in dismay and disarray as I watched her put the infants down right on the lip of the pool which seemed to bubble and steam even more. My hackles rose as the frightful scene unfolded close to me. The so-called mother jerked up each child by their heels, one in each hand and held them squirming over the steaming surface. I closed my eyes to blot out the horror as she began lowering the two kids headfirst into the boiling water, holding tightly onto their ankles. There was a sudden splashing, then silence followed by the sound of something hitting the surface of the water. I opened my eyes and the two tiny babes were nowhere in sight.

'There it is done and I am undone,' she shrieked beyond herself, and turned on me her eyes flashing with madness. 'Go, you ugly mongrel; go and join your savage mob. Get, or do you prefer to join them in that pool where another went before them. Go on, jump in and be an elder brother to them, mingle your flesh with their flesh in a oneness that has been denied me. It is done, but not over with,' she shrieked again. 'Where is that old savage that came and destroyed my home. There is nothing here for me now and soon there shall be nothing anywhere for him. I shall be revenged,' she screamed. 'Where is he? Is that the sound of his clacking sticks and harsh chants? Where is he? I'll rend him apart, rip the legs from his trunk, then his arms. No matter how old he is, I'll tear off his head and with my teeth, I'll bite off his genitals and let his blood gush like a fountain into my mouth. Who cares if it stinks with the vinegar of old age. I'll drain him dry!'

I panicked and sprang to race away, but got entangled in my legs and fell at her feet. I panted softly, waiting for her to dispatch me into the boiling pool. She was bending over me. Her mad red eyes were riveted on me. Her fangs were emerging from between the redness of her lips. She reached out to me and I couldn't help myself, I licked her hand as it came within range of my tongue. But her hand continued moving and to my neck. It ruffled the hair there as she smiled grimly and said: 'You are my dog and have tasted my blood. You are mine forever.'

I didn't want to be this thing's doggy anymore, no matter how much I liked her hand on me. Why, since I had been down here she had not even fed me. All this talk of blood had made me aware of my own hunger; but I knew I wouldn't get anything from her while she was on the warpath and out of her mind. I got to my feet, shivering all the while in deadly shock, though I put it down to my weakness from hunger, and my legs by their own accord propelled me away from that mother who had killed her own children. Her mocking laughter followed me as I raced away to where I hoped to find my shaman father – he would save me from this terrible witch and hopefully give me a feed too.

CHAPTER FIFTEEN

A dog can take just so much from a beloved mistress or master and I had had enough, at least for the time being, racing away from her as fast as my legs could move me. Even this, I considered not as rapidly as I wished to go and sought the air for added speed. Before I realised it, I was skidding through the weird atmosphere of the vast cavern and just ahead there were two figures flying. With a yelp of joy, I bounded forward to where Goanna and Leopard were turning to welcome me.

Just as I thought I was safe from pursuit, from behind and below me came the shook-shook of giant bat wings. I strove for altitude, but as I rose I saw another flying figure above. Was it waiting for me? I gave a sigh of relief as I neared. It was a bandicoot and even then when danger threatened, my hunger leaped me towards it. The animal saw me coming at a great pace and took off with me after him. I didn't care what was happening behind. I wanted that warm body between my jaws. I loved bandicoot flesh.

But once alerted, the bandicoot was quick with a nervous energy that sped him to the roof or what might be called the sky of the cavern. He flashed through a circular opening, much like the entrance to a burrow, and it was then that I pulled up unwilling to be trapped within; but then the voice of my father came into my head urging me and Leopard to go on. 'You and Leopard go into that opening. It leads to the outside. I'll stop that creature from following after you, for above it is night and it knows this.'

I didn't wait another second, for if my father told me to go into that burrow I would, and then that was where that bandicoot had gone and I wanted it. Up and up I rushed with Leopard coming on behind me. As I rose, two voices in my head battled to possess me. My father urged me to flee and my mistress called me to return; but ahead of me was that flying hunk of meat, Bandicoot, and I was ravenous for it. When I was stuffed full, then and only then would I think about going back, though that was doubtful, for what dog wanted to live only on rancid fish, or for that matter, what human wanted only to live on mushrooms and rancid fish?

'Come back, come back,' she howled hysterically.

'Hungry, hungry,' I barked back, not knowing if I could do the mind talking thing myself.

'Come back, come back,' she shrieked again, then turned her voice on my father. 'You old man or lizard, or whatever rubbish you are, get out of my way, I have no time to deal with you.'

Ascending straight up a chimney did not need much in the way of manoeuvring and I looked over my shoulder. Leopard snarled in my face, but I could see past him. Far below was the circle of white which was the exit from the cavern, then something blocked out the light. Whatever it was, it was as huge as the mouth and perhaps was rushing up the chimney towards me. I tried for more speed as her voice filled my mind.

'What, flash light at me and expect me to burn? Fool, what crystal can harm me here,' the banshee howled. 'There, I direct it back at you. Let it eat away your withered flesh and, and ... What, stone? You are stone! Get out of my way. No, no, you are blocking up that tunnel like a cork. Well, you old fool, remain stone! I have many exits and whether I reach them this night or some other, I shall eventually, you know.'

With a high-pitched scream which seemed strong enough to shatter the plug which prevented her from getting after us and which did vibrate alarmingly in my mind, the creature turned, for now I was seeing through her eyes. She fled shrieking across the vast deserted cavern and into the grotto which had been her home. Like some giant moth, she fluttered from wall to wall. How pathetic were the mats of moss there. She shrieked again and then with a steady shook-shook of her great leathern wings, she hurtled through the cavern and into a tunnel which angled down into the bowels of the earth. Then I could see nothing through her eyes and the only sound was the shook-shook of her wings steadily beating through the darkness with a constancy and determination which boded ill for us. Thankfully, then the connection broke as I surged upwards and out into the above-ground where the dawn sky was lightening my world so that I could see about me and down where a number of wallaby were huddled. I hurtled down upon one which had only enough time to throw a startled glance up into the sky before I was ripping at its throat. I assure you that that was one of the most satisfying and tasty meals I have ever eaten. It does pay to regulate your appetites, for when you do, it's a fine night when you satisfy them fully and utterly.

CHAPTER SIXTEEN

'Without Jangamuttuk and Ludjee, I won't go,' Hercules shouted, though this time his club did not thud down onto the ground. He was faced with something he could not bash into submission.

We were back on the island; but without my father and mother. An air of despondency hung over our mob. They wanted to wait for their missing members, while our chief mate had decided to press on while conditions were favourable. 'At last, the wind is right, blowing steadily from the east. We can't wait here, it is too dangerous. Jangamuttuk and Ludjee will meet us along the coast. He sent me ahead to get our vessel underway,' he told them abruptly. Since his escape from the underground, he had little patience with ordinary people, even his best friend, me, George. 'Your shaman ordered me to take you west and I'll take you west, but, well, suit yourself.'

'Well, you suit yourself and go,' shouted Hercules, and this time his club did thud down on the ground. 'You go on with the mob and I'll find them and meet you along the way. Keep watch and when you see our smoke, come in. We began this voyage together with Jangamuttuk and Ludjee as our guiding lights and it is only right that we finish it with them in our midst.' Down again went his club and without another word he strode off to the causeway. As he reached it, he shouted back over his shoulder: 'Just let that Strongarm get in my way.'

'If anyone else wishes to go with him, then go,' our captain said dourly. 'If not, get on board for we sail within the hour.' And he marched off to the boat.

All of us trailed after him. We were learning to obey his commands and it was then that we stopped seeing him as our chief mate and accepted him as our captain on whom we had to rely if we were to reach the end of our voyage. This, alas, proved to be putting our hope in a false leader, though by the time we discovered that, it was too late for most of us.

We were soon all aboard, running hither and thither as he barked out commands. Previously as we had got underway, there had been the voice of our shaman raised in song; now he had gone and taken with him our sense of well being. We went about our tasks gloomily. Still, the wind was fair and to the west. Quickly our sails were set and we were bowling along at a rapid pace keeping up with the whitecap waves which rushed along at our sides, but many of us including myself cast our eyes back where we had left the two guiding lights of our voyage, my father and mother. I admit that I cried as we left the land behind and with it my childhood. I had become as an orphan, but then I was old enough to bear it, except for those betraying tears streaming down my face.

And so we continued sailing on in that numb emptiness which comes to the soul when your spiritual helper is gone. This made our voyage a melancholy affair, though the days were sunny and the nights bright. Sometimes in the deepest part of the night when we lay awake brooding over our misfortune, there came the faint sound of clapsticks and the raspy chanting of our shaman's voice; but then the reality of our sails shuddered and gave out a shook-shook sound like the rattle of deadmen's bones which overwhelmed any imaginary voice and made whoever was at the helm cling to the wheel in mute desperation. Sometimes, when I stood by our captain, Wadawaka, when the shook-shook surrounded us like the swooping of giant bat wings, I saw his fist clench on the helm until the whiteness shone through the black.

His good spirits were a thing of the past and he rarely spoke about anything which did not have something to do with the smooth sailing of our schooner. He kept our vessel heading straight towards the west and she never deviated from our course; on our starboard the coast stretched on and on in an arc which we chorded. Even though, every now and again a plume of smoke rose, Wadawaka never investigated them. It seemed that my mother and father had dropped completely from his mind.

Our captain could not remain all the time at the helm, nor could he continue to invent tasks which supposedly kept our schooner seaworthy. Indeed such was the fineness of the weather and the constancy of the breeze that she ran along her course with the minimum of supervision. It was then, when he had exhausted all that he could think to do, he found another sort of work. He began carving a log of wood which he had taken from the island. This he first hacked into the rough shape of a human figure, then began gently to chisel out the smooth contours of a woman's body. As the wood shaped, I saw that it was in the likeness of our mistress. I wondered why he did this, for he should have been, as I was, more than happy to leave her and the underground imprisoned in the vaults of his unconscious mind; but it was not his way and I observed how he took a grim joy in rendering the naked body and features of the female creature that had called herself his wife and who I had rashly considered my mistress. Such delusions, I thought as I stared at his large black hands smoothing out the creamy wood and creating anew that well remembered face. I stared at it and suddenly my old yearning was back in all its strength. I sought to thrust it away and out from me. She had destroyed my mother and father, and I was in mourning for them, so why should I yearn for her? I decided then that she had stolen my soul, but this did not lessen my longing for her. And with this yearning for her came also the feeling that my parents were still alive and that she had not severed them from me. It was then that I knew that Hercules would find them and we would meet again; but still I doubted this as I stared at the wooden image and saw those eyes glaring at me as my once friend, Wadawaka, coloured them in.

Once I had been a confused dog, now I was a puzzled human filled with conflicting emotions that should not have been there, hence my belief that she had stolen my soul. I wanted my parents back as well as wanting my mistress, though I was no longer a dog, but George, a human. Perplexed by these longings, I went to the side of the schooner and stared across at the distant coastline. If only Hercules' column of smoke would rise to bring us a happy reunion. But there the land lay, flat and featureless. No hills or mountains broke the flatness, as we were sailing off the southern coast of this desert where we now are searching for the yellow metal. Yes, even then I pictured this desert nothing and imaged Hercules and my parents trying to cross it and he dying of thirst. His only chance of survival lay with us and our schooner; but here was our ruthless captain, brooking no delay as he rushed to the west.

What was wrong with us, what had we become, I thought as I turned my attention to the waves slapping our vessel's flanks as she rushed through them. I looked about the deck where others of our mob lay or stood, as I had done, staring at the monotonous waves. Now I slumped to the deck and lay in the warm sun trying to forget my parents and Hercules. We could do nothing to help them if they did not send their column of smoke up into the sky, so why waste time and linger along the coast when my father, Jangamuttuk, had his heart on us finishing our voyage with or without him.

Then I fell into other thoughts, of her hand on me and I moaned softly along with the wind blowing gently through our rigging and the whitecapped waves rocking me so tenderly. For once I was at peace and might have remained so believing that what adventures I had had were but the result of my father's drugs. Even my time as an involuntary dog seemed but a hallucination and I had no desire to test the reality by becoming Dingo. I held to my human shape and even began feeling that such things as Dreaming animals were pure imagination, for Wadawaka remained Wadawaka and shape-changing was only an adolescent dream. We were human and as humans could not leave our schooner and fly over the land seeking Hercules and my parents.

Our rush west was necessary, for our schooner was old and worn and could not remain seaworthy much longer. Wadawaka's skill and determination had kept her afloat and shipshape. Under his compulsion to see that everything was in order, the last of the canvas we had gleaned from the wreck had been stretched to billow in the wind. It was well that he had fixed everything and that there was no change in the fine weather, for when he turned his attention to his image, he neglected his vessel. Finally, after days of carving and smoothing, the figure was as finished as it would ever be. He stared at it awhile, altered a curve here and there, then stated to himself, 'It will do!'

I had been hurt when our captain, who used to be my best mate, had stopped confiding in me; but when I saw that he never spoke much to anyone except to order them to do things, I left him alone. I thought that he would come around in time when the shock of what he had suffered underground, whether real or hallucination, had worn off. After all a diet of magic mushrooms did implode the mind and then such was the mood of our ship that none of us spoke much anyway. We lacked our singer of songs who had lifted our spirits when they were down. Now they slumped and there was no-one to lift them up, and not even that sometimes distant – perhaps imaginary – sound of clapsticks could do so. In desperation we clung to the hope that along the way Jangamuttuk and his wife would join us, but as the days fled past, even this hope died. What marked the end of this increasingly forlorn hope was the day when Wadawaka lifted his figure and, hugging it to his broad chest, took it to the very bow of our schooner where after a good deal of effort he fastened it beneath the bowsprit.

'There,' he declared to himself, though we could not help but hear. 'Now she has eyes to see and if I might I could rename the vessel, *Amelia;* but why, when I did name her the *Kore*. She is the *Kore* and will remain so, named after that vessel we plundered when she had sucked all aboard her dry. Sail on, sail on, maiden, for you are a thing of spite,' he exclaimed.

And I could not help adding, 'to where my mother and father wait for us.'

He stared at me and suddenly I saw what seemed to be a look of complete despair on his face. I couldn't believe it. Wadawaka had always been just as strong as my mother and father and now here he was looking as hopeless as I felt. I stared, examining him for other signs, but he spread his hands in a gesture that I had not seen him use before and replied to what had been a statement, rather than a question. 'Where what awaits us awaits us.' He then took the helm from my listless fingers; but we were aimed straight and true and he merely did so to avoid further conversation.

It was after he had placed the figurehead before us that our mood of melancholy deepened into despair. We hardly noticed, though Wadawaka did, when the westward extent of the land came to an end and it turned abruptly north. It was the end of the land and thus the end of our voyage. We should have greeted the end of our confinement on the schooner with a joyous party; our eyes should have been fastened on the shore where lay our promised land. This was what our shaman, and my father, had promised us and there it lay, rolling hills and forests so like our long lost home; but we merely gazed listlessly upon it, and strangely we viewed our future land with apprehension. Why, someone might have asked, though none did, for it all seemed as Jangamuttuk had said it would be.

Wadawaka took the wheel and steered toward the coast. When we could see the waves breaking upon the beach, he ordered our extra sails to be lowered and under our mainsail we crept along the shoreline. The breeze urged us along and we came to where the land went inland, then out to round about a bluff and extend north. Our captain took up his glass and examined the indentation. Seemingly satisfied, or deciding at last that we could go down this inlet, he gave me the wheel, then raised his glass and scoped out the land. We came in rapidly and with my unaided eyes I saw what he was closely examining. Towards one side of the indentation, there was a narrow passageway between tall cliffs which in all likelihood led either to a sheltered harbour or the outlet of a river in which we could anchor in safety.

He swept the surface of the water with his glass, then said: 'Deep, deep, it is deep enough.' He followed the cliff face along to the end where water and beyond that land waited for us. 'It will do, it will do,' he said lowering his telescope. It was then that the clouds which had been hanging low, descended and a light drizzle began falling. The sea turned sullen and the waves lost their white tops to roll heavily against the shore and through the passageway. Our vessel lifted and sank, lifted and sank. The hull creaked and our single sail shuddered and gave out a mournful 'shook-shook' as Wadawaka swung the helm. The schooner trembled like a living woman, lost her leeway in confusion, then turned towards the passageway.

Naturally, even though our spirits were low, we were all on deck. In fact, the sight of the land did excite us and most of my mob clustered at the bow where they waited to rid themselves of the schooner and the sea. They thought that once they had the solid earth under their feet all would be well. Some began pointing out blurred features of the landscape and others said that they could see, even though the fog blanketed everything, columns of smoke rising beyond the passageway. Those who could not see this said they could smell it. They were exchanging opinions in this way, when a wave got under our hull. We lifted up and the forepart of our vessel slid into the passageway and between the frowning cliffs.

It was then, when all were looking forward to the end of our voyage, it was then and I swear on it, though it surely must have been a hallucination, that the cliffs came together with a resounding crack. The bow of our vessel, and all my mob with it, was completely crushed. This happened so quickly that before I was barely aware of the catastrophe the walls came apart and the remaining part of our schooner, the stern, slid beneath the surface, taking us down with it. We went down and down until there was a rush of air and we popped up to be rushed through the passageway and into a fine harbour. The mist or fog lifted and even though I was in the water and in danger of drowning, I gave a gasp which might have turned into a mournful wail if my mouth had not instantly filled with water. I paddled furiously to stay afloat as my eyes took in what lay before us.

In front of us, here in what my father had called our promised land, was a sprawling ghost settlement with a dozen or so ships at anchor. It was then that I thought to give up my life and let myself sink beneath the waves; but Wadawaka grabbed me and towed me ashore. So our voyage ended with the loss of our vessel and all folks on her, except for two of us.

This might be a good place to stop my yarn, yet there is a little more to come about what happened to us after we were tossed ashore. Well, the dawn is still an hour off and I'll just tell you about those last events even though you're all nodding off about me into dreams of sudden wealth.

CHAPTER SEVENTEEN

We, the only two survivors, crouched on the sand of the beach in a sodden dismay as bedraggled and as wet as our bodies. If our minds had not been dulled by the sudden catastrophe, we would have shrieked our pain to the very heavens. Everything had been taken away: parents, now the ship and my mob. What else could I do, but follow after them to the fabled skyworld. Up there, I would meet them all again and voyage on that milky ocean that might indeed have a promised land on some far coast; but I hardly believed this and as for Wadawaka, who knew what he wanted to do?

We sat there in a sullen silence, not even lifting our heads to examine what was supposed to have been our refuge – some refuge all right, but for the ghosts, not for us humans. So my father had been mistaken about this and perhaps there were other things he had been wrong about. So, as from about the bay came the sounds of a busy ghost settlement, the ringing of hammers, the shouts of its inhabitants and the creaking of rowlocks from the boats plying to and from the dozen ships riding at anchor, I started to doubt the wisdom of my father. At last, I found the energy and spirit to lift my head. I stared at my once friend for support, but he was busily examining the ships. His eye settled on a dark low craft anchored some way off from the others. He stared at it until he finally felt my gaze on him and looked at me. If I was expecting succour from him, I was sadly mistaken.

'It is a sturdy whaling vessel from the Americas,' he told me, though I wanted words of comfort from him and perhaps even the offer to help me perform a ceremony for our mob. We had just seen our friends and relatives crushed and drowned in front of our very eyes and had almost suffered the same fate, and my father had always emphasized that when such a catastrophe happened it was up to the survivors to send the souls on their way to the skyworld; but all that Wadawaka could talk about was that ship. 'There it rests, but will soon commence its voyage, for the crew are busy at the sails. I have had this land,' he suddenly exclaimed almost in a shout, then his voice lowered, 'And I've had her and my fill of dreams. I will take berth on that whaler, for they are always looking for a complement to their crew,' he suddenly decided, ignoring me and my dilemma entirely. 'Their voyages are long and hazardous and this will be to my liking.'

It was then that he remembered his erstwhile friend and tried to place me in his plans. 'Perhaps, you too,' he said, 'should sign on and get away from all this. We listened too much to Jangamuttuk, that obeah man, supposedly your father, and his dreams of finding a place free of ghosts. Well, we sailed on the wings of his songs only to find them here. They are everywhere and we must accommodate ourselves to them. Come and join me, for I have taught you the ways of the sea and it will not be difficult for you.'

Well, at last he had considered me, but did I really want to sail my life away? I didn't like the looks of that vessel either. Why had it been moored in isolation away from the others and why did it look so restless to be off. I stared at the sinister whaler, then at the wide land back of the bay and made up my mind.

'Perhaps my parents are still alive,' I told him, 'and then there is Hercules. It would take a lot to kill that bloke. I'll find him and learn what has happened to my mother and father. I haven't got anything else to do, and without them, I don't want to live on,' I cried, my despair rising, for I doubted if they were still alive; but, as I said, it would give me something to do.

'Well, suit yourself, for I need the ocean after that spell underground and none of this creeping along a coastline, especially this one. I've had enough of the happenings here and want to set my hands to tasks I know. Such work I won't find in that settlement, then best that I avoid it. There is the matter of my being an escaped convict and, well, I am not sure of my freedom if I remain in this British colony. Best be gone while I can go,' he said, his voice breaking as a response to my own despair.

Our conversation had merely resulted in both of us feeling such a level of despondency that if we persisted in our misery the next step would be taking our lives. I had already attempted this in the water and might have tried to do something of the sort again, if the image of my mistress had not come into my mind. At least she was still alive and had petted me on occasion, though I still remember those pangs of hunger when I was with her. Still, the thought of her did lift my spirits a little. I stared at the cluster of huts and the few houses set in the familiar pattern which my father had seen as having some occult meaning, much like a spirit catcher. I finally struggled to my feet and began walking along the beach towards it. In truth, I didn't care if it had some such function or other: I had already lost my soul. Wadawaka, a companion to my misery, followed after me.

No-one took notice of our ragged appearance or colour as we followed the beach past the rows of huts, anchored at strong points by sturdy dwellings, and reached the jetty which thrust out into the bay. It was then that I noticed that there were other blackfellows about, dressed similarly in rags and sitting in a circle just above the beach and close to a substantial building, which seemed to be a ration depot. The dark eyes passed over us and returned to eye us furtively as we passed them and went onto the jetty where stood a heavy-set man dressed in a dark frock coat and a tall hat on his melon-shaped head. He was clean shaven and his eyes shifted over us without recognition. But, to our dismay, we recognised him. It was that Fada ghost who had had charge of the settlement far to the east where we had been incarcerated. He had finally deserted us, leaving us to our fate; I believe we would all have died there, but for stealing the schooner. A fat lot that had done us, for now except for a possible quartet of us, we were extinct.

My face dropped to my chest and I felt the tears come. I was becoming a regular crybaby and jerked my head up. Beside that Fada, in easy familiarity, stood a plump ghost girl dressed in lightish clothes which the wind pressed against her, showing her sturdy legs. On her head she wore a bonnet of straw with ribbons tied beneath her chin. She took no notice of us as if we were merely part of the scenery, though her companion held all of her attention. Her face was slightly upturned to that of Fada whose head was only an inch or two above her own.

When we stopped at the end of the jetty, Wadawaka hissed: 'What is he doing here? You know who that is?'

'Why it's that ghost, Fada, who placed us in that book of his, so that we died each time he numbered one of us.'

'Well, that is one way to put it, for he is a worthless one, but then he is more than that to you,' he replied pensively, staring at a whaling boat preparing to cast off. 'Well, since all your mob is gone, it does no harm to tell you that he is your natural father. You must have wondered why your skin was lighter; now you know.'

How many more blows could I take before I broke under them? I suddenly shuddered all over and could hardly get my eyes settled enough to stare at that stout ghost who had fathered me. My eyes jerked off him, then back again. I began noticing things about him in a series of disjointed images. His red hair not quite right, the shape of his hat, the whiteness of his face, the pudginess of his hands. 'But, but,' I managed to stutter forth to the person who had dealt me such a blow. 'Is he, is he?' I questioned in amazement. 'How could he be!' I demanded. 'He was against such things.'

'That may be, but he spent many nights with your mother and you came from them. Perhaps if you make yourself known to him, he will take you in charge; but suit yourself. I am aboard that yonder ship. It waits for me. I know it. Hey, you, sir,' he yelled at the man in charge of the whaling boat. And in return, he received a strange answer from another portly ghost who had a somewhat high piping voice. He addressed himself, saying: 'Is that a savage, addressing Starbuck, mate of yonder ship, and in English too. Well, perhaps he was a seaman cast adrift, or becoming drunk, ended up in this godforsaken place. Well, noble savage, answer me quickly, for we have finished our business yonder and are ready to cast off. Our captain is ever eager for the chase and it hurls us and him on to whatever waits beyond the horizon, which is, as he's told us time after time, what is huge and white – but that is no matter for you. Answer quickly, uncouth savage, what do you wish of Starbuck?'

'To join the crew of your ship.'

'Do you know the whaling business; can you pull an oar, and lastly are you ready for our captain?' Starbuck retorted back strongly.

'I know the business; can pull an oar with the best of them, and as for captains, they are more or less the same, masters of the brigs they command.'

'But this captain is beyond all other captains. Know ye that this is the *Pequod*, named after a vanished savage tribe. Beware, it may prove too savage for you savage and lead to your extinction.'

'I have had savage masters beyond savagery.'

'But I dare say, not of this ilk, for his savagery is within. Well, hop down and take that oar, we'll see how you pull. Slacken and over the side you go. We are out with the tide and shall brook no delay.'

I watched as my once friend, without a backward or sidewards glance, leapt down into the boat to settle himself at an oar. Starbuck gave the order to pull and the four oarsmen bent their backs and sent the craft skidding across the water. My friend's eyes lifted with every backward stroke and I saw a sign of farewell in them and I swear that his lips mouthed the words: 'In time we'll meet again'.

We indeed had been through a lot together and the final agony had been the loss of crew and schooner. Indeed it was a heavy blow for a captain to bear and he was bearing it perhaps worse than I knew. I too was bearing it badly, for again those sad tears were dribbling down my cheeks as the boat reached the vessel's sides and was lifted – men and all – straight up on the deck. All was bustle, though not confusion as she prepared to depart. Abandoned by all, I stood on the jetty staring at the whaler. I heard clearly across the water, Starbuck's piping voice detailing aspects of the whaler which looked like no vessel should. It was a fetish thing of wood and bone, such as I had seen in one of Fada's books.

I listened on, for I wanted to know what my erstwhile friend had chosen. 'This will be your home if the captain agrees,' Starbuck spoke. 'And note what sort of home it is. Look around and examine the curious fittings. You may have your savage craft covered all over with devilish designs, but not as this. Note the quaintness of both materials and devices gleaned from her calling. See those open bulwarks garnished with those long sharp teeth so that it bears a canny resemblance to that of our prey, which is that king of all that swims in the briny ocean. I mean, you ken, the sperm whale. And see the helm on the quarter deck. Observe it closely, not an ungainly wheel, but a tiller and see from what it is made. Why, it is the long narrow jaw of that selfsame sea beast; but wait, here is our most curious artefact. It is our captain. Note the black storminess of his brow and if you think you can bear it, wait for he stands beneath that golden doubloon fastened upon the mast. There is a story within that piece and as everything else about this ship, it narrates but the story of that whale. Now, he comes. Hist and let him ramble, then you're the man for him, and if you are, all I can add is: God save your heathen soul.'

A clicking came to my ears which resembled nothing else, but that of my father's clapsticks. Father, did I say? Father in his care, but not in life, for that ghost behind me had sired me and tainted me with his phantom blood.

Then broke into my thoughts a self-loathing, stern and unyielding. It was the captain's voice. 'A ragged savage! Am I to add another savage to our complement? Come ye then and answer me this: do you wish to join me in my quest? But stop, don't reply as yet. Know ye not, oh savage, we hunt the white whale. It was he that took this leg and in taking it he took my soul. Now, in exchange, I will relieve him of both life and soul. What do ye think of this, if think ye can. No thoughts, no thoughts, look! The captain before you and there, that shining circle of gold. Join me and it may be yours.'

'I join you for I too would hunt leviathan.'

'You would, eh? But first my other savages. Here, Queequeg, there Dagoo, Tashtego and that lurking thing there, the Parsee, Fedallah. Can thou cast thy lot with these and send the lance hurtling into the very jaws of Moby Dick, for it is him I pursue throughout the seven seas. I'll drink his blood as I quaff fine wine.'

'I have known blood drinkers before and find them not to my liking, still, I can abide it as long as it is not my blood. If they wish, let them do so, I say. And these are your harpooners, similar to my own shade of skin. I'll cast my lot and my spear along them. Have you one to hand?'

'This is the deadliest one, tempered in leviathan's blood. How I wish it was he. Now show me, show me that ye can smite that whale!'

There came a little quiet, then a sudden whang that echoed over the water and startled the female beside the father ghost.

'By God, savage, you may have struck your mark, but if it had been his eye it would still be glaring.'

'Sir I did not wish to pierce the coin. It must be whole for a purpose. I did not want to make change by driving it in half.'

'Well, that is consideration and such consideration makes you one of these savages, my harpooners.'

'He is an African, sir, not a savage. His features are similar to mine and perhaps how he came to these shores, bears the telling,' another voice cut in.

'Better the telling of how he smote the whale. I feel that his black skin is stained by the blackness of his heart. I want his rage, not the story, and usage of it against leviathan.'

'Sir, I do rage against that which is huge and white and oppresses us. It bears a flag ...'

'Flags are but rags, bar the scarlet pennant denoting the rampaging fish, that is flag indeed. Starbuck, see that he is clothed in better gear, then set him to work. Unreef the sails now. We sail to fight our fright and bring him low.'

Soon the sails were billowing and the anchor, hoisted up, swung dripping pearls of water at the bow of the ship. I watched her move, carrying off my friend. She headed straight for the passageway that had been our doom. Tears flowed again from my eyes, for he had taught me the way of the sea and I could have held my own among that crew. I should have gone with him, but it was too late. I watched the ship, a thing of fluid motion, sail straight between those rocky cliff faces.

It was then that the short stout ghost, my supposed father, came past me with nary a glance and, with his woman on his arm, went to the very edge of the jetty to gaze over the waters.

'There is nothing finer than a ship under full sail,' he pompously declaimed in that well known voice.

'And there is nothing sadder than a woman who has lost her husband, sir,' an equally familiar voice spoke behind me.

I turned, confronting a figure all in black. Her body which I had only seen naked was covered from neck to feet in a long black dress and even her hands were hidden by black gloves as was her face behind a veil falling from a wide-brimmed black hat.

Conflicting emotions overwhelmed me. I stood there petrified and she whispered one word, 'Dog', and I felt myself changing. I stood in the puddle of my rags, then, overjoyed not to be alone, bounded to her side just as the ship disappeared from view. It was then that Fada and his young female turned. They stared at the woman all in black with the large brown dog squatting at her side.

'Madam, allow me to introduce myself,' Fada said, being very much the gentleman. 'I am Sir George Augustus and this is my wife, Lucy, the light of my life. We have been lately wed and this is more or less our honeymoon, though I am on official business under appointment to the Colonial Office.'

He swept off his hat and bowed. The dark figure before him, rested one hand on my head as she murmured in reply: 'Sir, pleased to make your acquaintance, I am Amelia Fraser and have had adventures here in this land that no mortal woman should have had thrust upon her; but thankfully trust in providence enabled me to survive. And, and this is my dog, I call him George, though I mean no disrespect. It is but a common name, since our late King passed on.'

And so the next portion of my adventures began. I had lost my complete mob and family to end up in what was to have been the promised land with the very man, supposedly my father, who had been the reason why we had fled in the first place. Strange indeed were the ways of our ancestors and I gave thanks as I trotted beside my mistress as she walked with Fada and his wife back to their quarters in Government House. I hoped that this time she would feed me well, especially as now she was in a much better mood since leaving that underground.

'A native dog, is it not?' Fada queried, then answered himself. 'They are said to be quite timid, but this one appears bold enough in its tameness.'

'It is indeed,' my mistress replied. 'It is indeed.'

And with these words, I must end my tale. The sun is lurking just below the horizon and my storytelling has given me a thirst which I must relieve before daybreak. I am sorry that I have kept you up, but out here in this wilderness, how else to pass the time but by detailing adventures strange and phantastic. My adventures continued, but there is no time left and I must end my tale with my entry into the promised land. Perhaps, I will return to continue my story, though I am for the north and leave today. Perhaps, if I have the time, I should put my adventures down upon paper so that a wider audience may marvel at them. I can write you know, for my father taught me when he was commandant of that mission far to the east. Well, I am at an end and Good Night, or should I say Good Morning. Whichever it is, I leave you to your fossicking. Good fortune to you all!